PRAISE FOR JOANNA BLAKE

Couldn't put it down. Can't wait to see if Mason gets a story and how things turn out for the family.

— AMAZON REVIEWER

Love her stories and the suspense of wondering what will happen. You can get lost in this fantasy world of love, heartache and happy endings.

— AMAZON REVIEWER

Loved the way this author writes. Will continue to read her books. Love those military heros!

— AMAZON REVIEWER

MARKED BY THE DEVIL

Women always seem to fall into my lap. Until an innocent beauty crosses my path and wants nothing to do with me.

I'm one of the **Devil's Riders**, the inner circle of one of the biggest motorcycle clubs in California. My brothers and I live on the edge of society, and we like it just fine.

I'm swimming in easy women, but I'm easily bored. Then one day, I see her. Molly McRae. She's easy on the eyes and **sweet as pie**. All I want to do is **take a bite.**

From the moment I see Molly, I'm on a mission. **I chase her down** and learn her name. Then I begin my campaign to **make her mine.**

I want to **mark her.** I want to tattoo her silky skin and kiss away her tears.

Hell, I want to put my brand on her. My name. My ring.

And I won't stop until she's mine.

Marked By The Devil is Book 5 in *The Devil's Riders* series. Each book features a **new couple** with visits from old favorites. *Marked By The Devil* can be read as a standalone but will be more enjoyable if the entire series in read in order.

MARKED BY THE DEVIL

JOANNA BLAKE

❀ Created with Vellum

For Christina Cartner Youngren
Thank you for all that you do, your love of books, and most of all
your friendship. You inspire me every day and make me laugh. I am so
lucky to have you as a friend, and so are all the animals you rescue!
Xoxox,
Joanna

INTRODUCTION

This is the fifth book in the *Devil's Riders* series. This can be read as a standalone, but I recommend starting at the beginning. At this time, these books are exclusively available on Amazon.

Devil's Riders Book Order:

- *Wanted By The Devil* (Devlin's story)
- *Ride With The Devil* (Jack's story)
- *Trust the Devil* (Donahue's story)
- *Dance With The Devil* (Whiskey's story)
- *Marked By The Devil* (Callaway's story)

Don't worry, the *Devil's Riders* series is not over. Audiobook versions are coming soon!

Enjoy!

Xoxox,

Joanna

THE NIGHT IT ALL CHANGED

Callaway

"*N*ot tonight, ladies."

I felt a little guilty about all the disappointed faces, but I had somewhere to be. A birthday to celebrate.

And to be honest, I was kind of bored with the constant hooking up with the club girls. They were more than just easy. They were literally always available and down to do just about anything a truly perverted mind could think up. Some of the guys called them *skanks*, but I didn't think that was a nice way to talk about a lady.

Of course, that didn't mean I hadn't spent many a night fucking them stupid. Usually, two or three at a time. More than a couple of times, four. And twice, five.

Yeah, I'm kind of a legend around here.

Not just for the way I use my ink gun either.

I'm the latest addition to the inner circle of the club. I'd come up with Whiskey and had been brought inside on his word. Devlin, Jack, and Donahue all counted me as a brother. All the club guys were brothers in theory, but we were close brothers. Tight.

Blood brothers.

I hadn't had much of a family growing up other than my nana. My parents had been addicts, and both died young. Not before scaring the fuck out of me a bunch of times though.

It had been my phone call, after finding my mom lying in her own sick with a needle in her arm, that made my nana come and get me. She'd tried to protect me for years, but my mom had put on a good show for Child Protective Services. This was the final straw.

I'd been six years old but smart enough to call my nana, who called 911. She'd driven hours in the dead of night to sit with her grandson and speak to the EMTs and the police. They treated my mother's lifeless body like she was a piece of garbage, just something in the way to deal with. An inconvenience, not a person.

I'd had an aversion to cops ever since.

And a boatload of respect for my grandmother.

I could never disrespect *any* woman because of that respect. Yes, they were more or less interchangeable to me, sexually. But I never turned down a good time.

But lately, things were changing. Lately, I had not been feeling it.

I wanted more than a place to put my dick. That was easy. I needed more than that. It was sneaking up on me, but it was there. I was like an uncle to Becky and Whiskey's kid, and it started to give me the itch for one of my own.

Of course, that meant I'd have to find a woman worth staying home for. I could hardly imagine it, but maybe, just maybe, I was willing to put away my wild nights for one very lucky lady.

I could say my future old lady was lucky for a couple of reasons, but number one was my incredibly long . . . tongue.

Even before I was a full club member, I'd never been at a

loss for women. The guys all thought it was because I had a pretty face and some major ink. Some thought it was my piercings. Or the fact that I had a gigantic dick.

Nope. None of those things.

All I had to do to get a woman was one thing.

I just had to show her I could lick my eyebrows.

Oh yeah, my tongue was longer than most guys' cocks. And I could work miracles with it. Of course, I didn't treat just anyone. But now and then, I'd show a lady a really, *really* good time.

I held a fist in the air as I left the clubhouse. It was still early, but there were women lining up, looking for fun. I had a bag of coke in my jacket pocket, a bunch of rolled joints, three bottles of tequila and a case of beer at my crib, but tonight, I was going to be a good boy.

Tonight was Nana's birthday.

I jumped on my ride and tore off, making sure to stop home to pick up the present I'd bought for her earlier. I'd had just enough time to swing by the fancy florist in town before they closed.

I headed to the skilled nursing home where my nana was living. I paid for every cent of her care, and it was expensive too. But she was worth it.

Because of the house I had bought her a few years back and all the money I'd sent her over the years, she didn't quite qualify for low-income medical insurance. So it was all out of pocket.

It was a good place, though, and she liked it. And if she ever took a fall again, someone would be there to help her. I'd nearly lost my mind last year when she took a tumble and was too far from the phone to call for help.

If I hadn't stopped by because of a weird, twitchy feeling

in the back of my mind, well, she might have lain there overnight. She was alone on the bathroom floor for a couple of hours as it was.

I doubted I would ever forgive myself for those hours.

I parked in the lot and pulled off my helmet. I ran a comb through my hair too, just to be respectful. Thankfully, Nana had never objected to my leather and ripped denim, but she did tell me to comb my hair every time I forgot.

She never criticized me or called me a delinquent, even though I clearly was. A successful delinquent with my own shop, but still, I was not exactly a Boy Scout. Far from it.

I'd started acting out in school early. Even later, when I wised up about keeping my mouth shut, I was up to no good. I'd been chasing, and being chased, by girls and even women from the moment puberty hit. I was tall for my age and already had a bad attitude. Then I'd discovered drugs and alcohol. If I hadn't learned how to use a tattoo gun, who knows what would have become of me?

If it weren't for Nana, I know what would have happened. Nothing good, that's for damn sure.

She'd loved me through all the bad times and the good. Now it was my turn. And damn if I wasn't going to do my best to make her final years the sweetest.

I nodded to the lady at the front desk. She knew me. They all knew me here. I kissed the cheek of a white-haired lady who passed by on her walker. I was pretty sure her name was Eloise, but I couldn't be sure.

She might smile like that at everyone, but it was such a sweet smile, so I always gave her a little kiss.

Nana's door was open, signaling that she was open for visitors. I always had a moment of worry right before I walked in. Worry that she'd be hurt or lying on the floor. Or worse yet, that she'd be gone.

But she was there, sitting in her favorite easy chair with her feet up, her bed neatly made (by the staff, I suspected) and a cup of warm tea on the little side table we'd brought from home. Most of the stuff in here was hers. It was like a little time capsule of her house and her life.

There was even a photo of my parents together on one of their rare sober days.

"Hi, Nana."

She used the side lever to lower her legs and waved me over.

"Get in here, you rascal."

I bent down to give her a kiss and got my cheek squeezed for my troubles.

"Woman, how are you so strong?"

She giggled like a school girl.

"What do you have there?"

"This?" I held up the flowers and present. "This is for an adorable woman who lives here." I pretended to look around. "If only I could find her."

She swatted at me and cackled. But her eyes were shining as I handed over the gift and sat on the edge of her bed, holding the flowers.

She opened the gift and crowed when she saw it was the latest book from her favorite author. She loved murder mysteries. I had teased her for years for being so bloodthirsty. She'd even had a murder mystery book club for a while.

I'd never seen anything like it. Six sweet as pie, white-haired grannies sitting around and talking about gory murders. It was too funny.

"Oh, there you are! Come in, sweetheart."

I turned my head in time to see a young woman tentatively waiting just outside the door. I saw dark, wavy hair, an exceptional figure, and the prettiest damn face I'd seen in my life. My entire life. She looked like a doll, with tawny skin and pink, luscious-looking lips.

But it was the huge, shy, deep blue eyes that caught and held my attention.

She was *too* pretty. Too sweet. Not to mention, she looked innocent and pure. Which instantly made me want to defile her, and not just once, like usual. Maybe four or five times, just for starters.

And just like that, my dick got hard. In a nursing home. Even worse, in the presence of my granny. I barely even noticed.

"Oh. I didn't know you had a guest, Miss Bonnie. I'll come back later."

I was too dumbstruck to do more than stare. The woman —the girl—was . . .

She was *perfect*.

And she was leaving. I stared as she backed out of the room, taking her rolling tray of books with her.

"Now that's the kind of girl you should be settling down with, my boy."

My first thought was:

She can't be real.

My second thought was:

She's way too good for me.

But I didn't say any of that out loud. Nana would have a fit if she heard me talking like that. She'd always told me I was as good as anyone else, and I agreed with her. Until now. That girl was . . . unearthly. She looked like a literal angel. I started praying that she had a gambling problem. A shoplifting addiction. A fault. Any fault. Anything that might put her remotely in my league.

I'd never gone out with a 'good girl'. I'd imagined them to be high-maintenance, bad in bed, and full of annoying rules. But for the first time in my life, I didn't care. I wanted the good girl, and I was going to get her, come hell or high water.

"What's her name?"

Granny tilted her head to the side.

"Oh, shoot. It's on the tip of my tongue."

I cleared my throat.

"I'll be right back."

She laughed and clapped her hands together.

"Go get her, Son!"

I ran down the hallway, looking around. I didn't see her anywhere, and I wasn't sure whom to ask. My heart sank. I was starting to wonder if I'd imagined the whole thing. After twenty minutes, I was walking in circles, not willing to leave until I got her name.

And then I heard it.

Singing.

I knew it was her before I was even close. When I looked in the open doorway, I stopped, frozen in place. She was singing an old church song, something I hadn't heard in years. A song that I'm sure I would have found dull if I'd heard it under any other circumstances.

She looked like an angel.

She sang like an angel.

And from the way she hovered over the young man laying immobile in that bed, she was literally an angel.

I was still standing there when she finished her song. She looked up and saw me, taking a tiny step backward. Dammit. I didn't want her to be afraid of me.

I remembered how I looked suddenly, covered in tats and wearing leather. And she couldn't even see all my piercings.

What was I doing? I must be insane. But that didn't stop me.

Nothing could.

"What's your name?"

"Me?"

I cracked a smile at that. Who else would I be talking to?

"Yes, you."

"Molly. Are you Bonnie's son?"

"Grandson. She raised me."

"Oh. She's a nice lady."

"Yeah. She's the best."

I watched her nervously take the man's hand. I frowned. Was that her . . . boyfriend? No, he was too young. And she worked here. *Move on, Cal.* A boyfriend wouldn't matter. Only a husband might stop me from what I was planning.

Maybe.

I cleared my throat.

"I'm Callaway."

She smiled but it wasn't a very big smile. That was okay. I realized I was going to have to move slow. She wasn't some club girl who was going to peel off her panties just because I snapped my fingers.

I almost moaned at the thought of this beauty docilely taking off her panties for me. I wondered suddenly what color they were. White, probably, I decided.

And just like that, white was my new favorite color.

"Do you work here? Or are you visiting?"

I nodded toward the young man on the bed. It seemed like an innocent question but she looked upset the moment the words left my lips.

"Both." She swallowed. "I work here to help pay for Tommy."

"Oh. You're a good . . ."

I was about to say 'friend' but I needed to know. I let my words dangle, hoping she would fill in the blanks.

"Sister."

I exhaled a sigh of relief. I was going to get this girl, and nothing would stop me. But even I would feel guilty taking her away from someone in a coma.

I wasn't a total fucking monster.

I was *willing* to be, if it got me what I wanted, but I would feel bad about it.

"How long have you guys been here? I've never seen you before."

I was grinning at her dopily. At least she didn't look like she was going to run off anytime soon. Of course, I was kind of blocking the doorway.

"We just got here a few weeks ago. He had an accident a few years ago. He was in a state-run hospital for a while but it closed down. I . . . I didn't know where to take him."

I realized the poor girl was about to cry.

"This is a good place. Try not to worry."

She nodded and gave me a brave smile. That smile just about broke my heart. In fact, I felt like my chest had cracked open and all these unfamiliar feelings poured out of me.

I felt protective. Possessive. And wildly turned on.

What the hell was wrong with me? Women were a dime a dozen. But that way of thinking made zero sense to me right now. Staring at her. Wanting her. Fucking worshipping her.

"I'd better get back to work."

"Do you need a ride home? I can wait. Nana is reading, but I can hang out a while."

She looked startled but she shook her head rapidly.

"I work the night shift." Then she gave me a shy smile. "But thank you."

I watched her push her cart into the hallway, fighting the urge to ask her what time in the morning I should pick her up.

Then I decided, fuck it. I'd just ask at the front desk and surprise her.

Molly. Her name was Molly.

CHAPTER ONE

Callaway

I sat on my ride, letting the motor idle. It was six AM and I was outside Nana's nursing home, waiting for Molly. I'd spent the night at home alone, not drinking and not doing much of anything.

I'd slept a little, but mostly, I'd lain in bed and stared at the ceiling, deep in thought.

I'd thought about my past. I'd thought about the present, which was an empty wasteland full of motor oil, tattoo ink, and easy women. The bright spots were hanging with my brothers and their families. My present that was hopefully about to change.

But mostly, I'd thought about the future.

I wanted Molly in it, whatever that looked like. I was far from the settling down type, but in the past few hours, I hadn't been able to imagine a future with her not in it. Not that I was picturing white picket fences. But I was thinking about having the girl in every damn way, as often as humanly possible.

Hell, I wanted to impregnate her. It didn't make sense, but some animalistic part of me wanted to maker her flat belly grow round with my baby. Either way, though, I wanted to go to pound town.

I figured that seven or eight times a day would take the edge off.

I'd never fantasized like that about a woman. I'd never had to. I'd been swimming in tail since I hit puberty. The truth was, I'd been the most popular boy in grammar school, too.

So all of this was out of character for me, to say the least. But I couldn't fight the overwhelming urge I had to claim her as my own. To mark her. To take her.

It wasn't just a sex thing, though that was a big part of it. I wanted to empty my balls into her so badly it made me break out in a cold sweat. But it was more than that.

It was a primal, caveman type of thing.

And that was after spending five minutes with the girl. I had no idea if I would have the same reaction to her in the light of day. I could hardly wait to find out.

So I waited. After a few minutes, a slight-looking girl appeared in the doorway. She glanced over her shoulder, waving at someone. Then she stepped out into the early morning light.

I stood up, putting the spare helmet under my arm. She didn't see me at first, so I took the time to have a long, thorough look at her. I was halfway hoping my memory had been exaggerating, embellishing her beauty.

But no. If anything, she was more beautiful than I could have imagined.

It was as if she was so perfect, my mind couldn't hold onto her image exactly right. Seeing her now, in person, well, it was like taking a long, cold drink on a hot day.

She closed her eyes and inhaled deeply, letting the misty air waft over her.

I cleared my throat, and she startled, sensing a predator.

She opened her eyes. They were the deep, rich blue of the sky at twilight, or an ocean wave right before it crested on the beach. She looked at me like a startled deer must look at a hunter.

I smiled at her without thinking. My instincts were to play it cool but I couldn't help it. Seeing her face just made me happy.

Fucking *absurdly* happy. Like a crazy person. Or a little kid who really, *really* wanted a red balloon.

"Hey."

CHAPTER TWO

Molly

I blinked at the mirage in front of me. I was tired, and I had a full day ahead of me. So for a minute, I was a hundred percent positive I was hallucinating.

There was a ridiculously good-looking guy on a motorcycle staring at me.

Good-looking, with chiseled cheekbones, a strong jaw, and a penetrating gaze. But dangerous-looking, with his fitted leather jacket and the tattoos peaking out at the top of his shirt and wrists.

He looked like a movie star. Like a modern-day James Dean, but even more dangerous. He looked like a Bond villain. A stranger.

But no. I did know him. I'd met him briefly, less than twelve hours ago.

Callaway. Bonnie's grandson.

How could I forget? The truth was, I hadn't. He'd flustered me badly the night before. I'd had a hard time not thinking about him throughout the long night shift.

I just hadn't expected to see him again so soon.

"Oh. Hi." I frowned. He was dedicated to his grandmother, I knew. Bonnie had told me all about him when I came back around with my book cart. But he'd just been here the night before. Surely, he wasn't coming twice in one week, let alone twice in one day? "What are you doing here? It's too early for visiting hours."

He smiled, and I almost took a step back. It was so blinding. The man looked like a *GQ* model, minus all that ink.

"Giving you a ride."

He held out the helmet, offering it to me. I stared dumbly at it, then back at his handsome face.

"Where to?"

"Huh?"

"You said you got off early, so I came back. You want breakfast? I know a good spot."

Oh, how I wanted to say yes. He made me nervous. But he was being so nice. And he was so very, *very* nice to look at.

But I didn't have time. I had to get to my day job. And I was so tired. I didn't have any room for distractions, especially one that looked like trouble.

Callaway looked like he knew everything about women and sex and lots of other things I should definitely stay away from. Meanwhile, I hadn't gone out with a boy since ninth grade. The year my folks died in an accident. The same accident that put my little brother into a coma. A coma he woke from briefly now and then and then almost immediately went back under.

My aunt had taken me in and helped with the paperwork to take care of Tommy. But when I turned eighteen, he had become my responsibility and my aunt had washed her hands of us.

She wasn't unkind. She just hadn't ever wanted kids of her own. And she had done her best for us without any actual enthusiasm.

After I moved out, she sold her little house and moved

down south. She wanted to be warm all year. She told me I had an open invitation to visit her.

A small, unkind voice in the back of my mind told me that she knew I never would.

She knew I would never leave Tommy. Never risk his waking up and my being so far away, not being there when he needed me.

All these thoughts passed through my overtired brain as the gorgeous, somewhat disreputable-looking man waited patiently for me to respond. It was probably less than a minute, but it felt like a lot longer to me.

"Oh. No. That's okay."

He tilted his head to the side.

"You got a ride? I can follow you to Mae's diner. It's real good."

I shook my head swiftly. I wished I had a car! It would have made my eighteen-hour workday a lot easier. Then again, I was usually so tired I was delirious. I caught lots of cat naps on the bus.

"No. No car."

His head remained tilted to the side, his eyes raking over me. But he didn't leer, like so many men did. He drank me in like his eyeballs had straws in them.

He was . . . intense. But not scary, which was odd, considering how he looked.

He stepped closer and I realized how tall he was. How big and how strong. He probably could have broken me in two. I still wasn't afraid.

Wary, yes. Skittish, but not frightened.

"Is it the bike? Is that what's bothering you?"

He ran his hand through his hair.

"No. I mean, yes."

He cracked a smile, and I was once again struck by how

insanely attractive he was. The man oozed sex appeal. Not that I actually knew a thing about sex!

"Which is it?"

"It's . . . I have to go."

"Okay. I'll drop you anywhere you want."

"I have to go to work. I—"

"Like I said, I'll take you. We can catch a raincheck on the food."

I had no answer for that. I stood perfectly still as he came closer, lowering the helmet onto my head. I broke out in chills at the gentle way he pushed my hair away and fastened the chin strap. I was mesmerized by the look in his eyes.

It wasn't just warm. It was blazing hot.

He took my hand and rubbed his cheek on it. I got shivers from the feeling of his skin on mine. It was so strangely intimate. Almost like he was a cat, wanting to be petted. He smiled at me, this time looking like a wolf. He squeezed my hand and tugged me toward the bike. 'Bike' was a laughably soft word for the giant metal machine he rode. I tried not to shiver when I saw the Devil's pitchfork emblazoned on the fuel tank.

"Where are we going?"

"Oakley's."

He nodded.

"I know where that is." He helped me onto the bike. "You always pull back-to-back shifts?"

"Yes. I mean, I take every shift I can get."

He frowned a little bit, then shook his head.

"That's a lot of work for a little girl like you."

He climbed on in front of me, then reached back to drag me against him. I gasped at the feeling of our bodies pressing together. It was by far the most intimate thing I'd felt in my life. And the smell of him . . . leather and oil and something else. Pine. He smelled like the woods on a cool autumn night.

I shook my head at that fanciful thought. Like I'd ever been in the woods at night!

I held on for dear life during the twenty-minute ride over to Oakley's. It was exciting and exhilarating. I was grateful for the cool wind in my face, which finally woke me up. Usually, it took me almost an hour to make the trip. I was actually early for my shift. This was definitely a much better way to travel.

I smiled in thanks as he helped me to my feet.

"Thank you for the ride."

"Can I see you later?"

I shook my head swiftly.

"I have to work."

He stared at me, his brows snapped together over his stormy green eyes. I was pretty sure he wasn't used to being told no. Not by anyone, let alone a girl.

"You're working tonight?"

I nodded, rubbing my arms. It wasn't cold out, but I hadn't worn a jacket. Tonight when I went home to shower before my shift, I would handle it. I'd dress warmer, I decided.

Maybe I'd even sleep a few hours.

"You've got to sleep sometime, girl."

I stood up straight.

"Molly."

He ran his knuckles over my cheek, and I shivered, swaying a little on my feet.

"You have to get some sleep, Molly."

"I'm fine. I should clock in."

I went to go, and he grabbed me, his hands firm on my shoulders. Then his mouth swooped down on mine. I inhaled sharply at the feeling of his lips. They were shockingly soft but firm. Insistent.

I gasped when I felt his tongue slide along my lips and jumped backward.

He stood there, a slow smile on his face.

"Dear God, I hope you're legal."

"What?"

"How old are you, sweetheart?" He held up his hand. "Actually, don't tell me. Lie. You are eighteen, right?"

I nodded slowly. What was he asking me?

"Are you really eighteen?" He shook his head. "I guess I do have a conscience, after all."

"Yes. Why?"

"Because if you weren't, *this* would be illegal."

He pounced on me, pressing me against the brick wall. His body pressed into mine. He seemed to mold into every soft part of me until we were one. I was shocked and elated at the same time.

His tongue dove into my mouth. It should have been gross but it wasn't. It was hot and tingly and fascinating. His tongue stroked mine, exploring my mouth. I felt my head fall back, and his lips were on my throat, sucking and licking and biting. His hands roved over my tee, up and down my back, until they settled on my bottom. He squeezed me and I let out a yelp.

"Please, don't stop me, sweetheart."

I pushed against him.

"I have to go."

He didn't move. He just leaned against the wall behind me.

"What time do you get off?"

"Seven," I blurted out.

"Liar. That's a twelve-hour shift. And the night staff at the home comes on at six thirty."

I glared at him. He was smart, damn him. I suddenly felt myself go limp.

"Four. I need to go home and sleep for an hour though."

He nodded.

"Okay. I'll pick you up."

I shrugged, the fight gone out of me. I didn't understand what was happening. A big part of me wanted to curl up against him like a cat and go to sleep.

But I needed this job.

"Do they have coffee in there?"

"No."

"Okay, I'll bring you one."

"I'm not allowed to have a drink at the register."

He ran his hands through his hair.

"What about lunch?"

"I usually catch a nap in the stock room."

"That doesn't sound safe."

I shrugged. He was right. It wasn't. I'd been undetected so far, but the store manager gave me the creeps.

"It's okay."

He stared at me, his jaw ticking.

"What time is lunch?"

"Oh, no, you can't come in the store looking for me. I could lose my job, and I'm already . . ."

"You're already what?"

"I just have a lot of bills."

He nodded and looked away, finally stepping back. He watched me straighten my clothes and look around. He was holding himself back from something, but what, exactly, I wasn't sure.

"Have a good day."

"I'll see you at four."

CHAPTER THREE

Callaway

Two jobs. No sleep. Alone.

This girl was going to kill me. Not just from the geyser ready to blow in my pants. She was going to make me lose my mind worrying about her.

How the hell she was still standing when I drove up to get her at four was beyond me. I'd though about going in there a dozen times and held back. I was already in over my head and all I'd done was kiss her.

But holy hell, what a fucking kiss it was.

She'd felt like an angel in my arms. A buttery-soft, sweet-smelling, supple, soft, and utterly feminine little package. A special fucking delivery, right to my gut.

I'd had a moment of panic when I realized she wasn't used to being kissed. Not that it made it any less sweet. But I had to wonder if she was of age. A girl who looked like her, well, it was hard to imagine she'd never been kissed.

But it *felt* that way. There was something untouched about her. And even though I was an outlaw, I wasn't about to go after an underage girl.

I remembered how Devlin had to wait for Kaylie. He'd nearly gone out of his mind, especially as the time drew near. If Molly had been seventeen, or even sixteen, well, hell . . . I had a feeling I would wait for her too.

But I would have lost my damn mind in the process.

There was no drug, no bottle, not even enough ink in the world, to take away this particular ache.

She stepped out of the double glass doors and into the parking lot. She shaded her eyes with her hand, blinking like a sexy little owl.

Hold up, Callaway. An owl? What the hell was happening to me? I slapped myself internally.

> *Get a fucking grip, Callaway. You've never once lost*
> *your mind over a piece of trim, no matter how*
> *hot she was. Why start now?*

But I had already lost my mind over this girl, and I knew it. And she was way more than a piece of ass to me. In fact, if anyone called her that, I had a feeling the guy would end up in the hospital. Or worse.

I walked over to her and pulled her in for a kiss. I did my best not to slobber all over her. She looked a bit surprised, but she didn't push me away. I winced when I saw how tired she looked. Not that she wasn't beautiful. She was. But her eyes looked weary and her face was pale.

"Come on, doll. Let's get you some rest."

"Okay."

"I'll get you tucked in and grab some food."

"Okay."

I grinned. I liked how agreeable she was being. Of course, she might just be too exhausted to argue. I knew I wasn't getting anywhere with this girl tonight. It wasn't like I was going to try and hump her while she was unconscious or anything.

"You working all night again?"

She nodded as I helped her with her helmet.

"And tomorrow?"

She nodded again.

"You're going to hurt yourself doing that. Tell you what—why I don't pull a shift for you? If they aren't paying you anyway, they won't care if you take a night off."

"No, you can't." She shook her head swiftly. "I need to be there in case he wakes up."

I sighed.

"But doll . . ."

She set her jaw and looked at me. She was no pushover, my little angel. I gave up, knowing I had to find a way to help her.

Not that it wasn't selfish of me. I mean if she never had a night off, I was not going to be having a lot of sex. And I wanted sex. All the sex.

But only with her.

Yeah, the candy shop had officially closed for business. Nobody was more surprised than me. But this slip of a girl had me tied up in knots, and I hadn't even had her yet.

If things kept going the way they were, I didn't see how I was going to get my dick wet in the next century. Something had to be done.

I'd talk to the guys, I decided. I wouldn't say anything about being head over heels. I'd act like it was no big deal.

Problem solved. Soon. I hopped onto the bike and guided her arms around my waist.

"Hold on tight, babe."

CHAPTER FOUR

Molly

I rolled over in my tiny bed, sighing in ecstasy. The bed was small and the apartment was dreary and drab, but right now, there was no place on Earth I would rather be.

A soft sound from the kitchen brought me fully awake.

I sat up, panic shooting through my body. I lived alone, in a not-so-great part of town. My landlord was a sweet old lady who had lived here with her family when it had been much safer. She'd turned the second floor of her house into two tiny apartments after her husband passed away. Right now, I was the only tenant.

I really liked Mrs. Keeley, but I couldn't exactly call out for help if I needed it. Not only could she not help, but I doubted she could even *hear* me. I glanced around for my phone, thinking I could call 911. Maybe they'd get here before I was dismembered. Or kidnapped.

Who was I kidding? Who would kidnap *me*? You needed family to pay a ransom, and it was pretty clear I didn't have any. If I did, I wouldn't be living in a place like this.

I held perfectly still as the sounds continued from the

kitchen. I heard a soft curse and sniffed the air. I frowned. Someone was trying to be quiet while they . . . cooked? It all came back in a flash. The huge biker who had started showing up last night. He'd driven me home and . . .

I closed my eyes, trying to remember. I blushed, recalling the way he'd kissed me and tucked me into my bed. He hadn't looked happy about letting me sleep, but he did.

I ran my hand through my hair and peeked into the kitchen. It wasn't far. The apartment was tiny, with a just a tiny bedroom and a kitchen big enough for a small table and chairs. There was the ancient bathroom that was surprisingly clean, a closet in the short hallway, and that was it. No living room. That was it.

Home, sweet, home.

And right now, there was a massive six-foot-tall man in leather and ripped denim, bending over the stove while a delicious smell wafted over to me. He looked up from what he was doing and smiled.

"Hello, beautiful."

He set down the spoon he was using on a folded paper towel and pulled me in for a kiss. A long, deep kiss that made me forget where I was for a minute. His lips were so warm and smooth. They molded to mine and then parted, his tongue slipping deep into my mouth. I kissed him back, tentatively at first, and then with an urgency I didn't quite understand.

"Damn!"

He'd lifted me slightly, I realized. My feet were dangling off the floor. He set me down gently and shook his head.

"Hmm. Damn."

"You said that already."

He just bit his lip and went back to the stove. The man

was too pretty for words. His dark green eyes were heavy-lidded and sensual-looking. His jaw could cut glass it was so sharp. And his lips were pink and soft. He was almost *too* good-looking.

I tried to focus, still feeling like I was half-asleep.

"You . . . cooked for me?"

"Stocked the fridge, too. Though to be honest, I don't much like the thought of you here all by yourself." He gave me a stern look. "This is not a good neighborhood."

He sounded like a mother hen. It didn't make sense with the tough and dangerous, sexy as all get-out image he presented. The man couldn't be real. Could he?

"Who are you?" I breathed, staring at him like he'd stepped out of a movie poster.

He cocked an eyebrow at me.

"Callaway." He gave me a cocky smile. "The guy who had his tongue down your throat a few seconds ago, remember?"

"First name?"

He leaned against the counter and crossed his arms. His thick, burly, muscled arms.

"Andrew. But nobody calls me that."

"Not even your grandma?"

He gave me a challenging look.

"No. She doesn't."

I hid a smile. He was lying. *Of course* his granny called him by his first name. At least sometimes.

"Okay, fine. But who *are* you?"

He crossed his thick, muscular arms over his chest. He looked resigned. Almost wary.

"Alright, let's do this. I ride with the SOS."

"SOS?"

"Sons of Satan. I'm their ink master."

"Ink?"

He shrugged out of his leather jacket and reached for his shirt. He gave me a look and hesitated.

"Might as well get this out of the way."

He pulled his black T-shirt up and over his head, holding it loosely in his hand. I barely noticed. I was staring at his chest. His arms. Everywhere.

He was covered in ink.

Literally covered in it.

"It's . . ." I reached out and traced the outline of a bird that looked like it was actually flying. It was so realistic. He flinched as my finger brushed his skin. "Beautiful."

He exhaled, staring down at me with a hard look on his face.

"You think so?"

I nodded breathlessly. I'd never seen anything like it. His entire upper body was tatted, but what tats they were.

It wasn't the usual skulls and daggers and snakes, though he did have a snake winding up one arm. This was more like a painting, with many elements woven together. Much of it was abstract, with some words here and there, references to Devils, and a scrawled *Live Free or Die* near his collarbone.

"You did this yourself?"

He nodded, watching me carefully.

"You're an artist."

"Tattoo artist, yeah."

"No, I mean . . . you are an artist."

He smiled brilliantly then.

"Thanks, babe." He kissed me again, his hands cupping my ass and squeezing. "Hmm . . . stop distracting me. You need to eat."

He gently pushed me toward the table.

"Sit."

I sat just as my stomach gave a loud rumble. I stared hungrily as he set down a plate of pasta, little twisty bows slathered in red sauce. There was a piece of bread on the side that smelled like garlic and olive oil.

I almost moaned in ecstasy.

"It smells amazing."

"Eat."

He sat across me and offered me a small bowl with grated cheese. I took a spoonful and shook it over my food.

"Italian food?"

He raised an eyebrow.

"Did you think Callaway was Spanish?"

I laughed, piling a fork high with food.

"No, it sounds English, I guess."

He grinned widely while I tried to eat with dignity. It was so tasty that it was difficult.

"Irish. I'm half and half."

He set a plate down in front of me.

"But I don't know shit about cooking Irish food. Nana's second-generation Italian."

"She taught you how to cook?"

He nodded. The man could cook, ride, he was a wizard with a tattoo gun, and he hadn't pressured me for sex. He'd let me sleep. I looked away, not sure how I felt about any of this.

That will teach you to judge a book by its cover, Mols.

He ran his hand through his hair and then laid it on the table. I stared at his inked knuckles. His chest was still bare and his gaze was too direct.

"When can I see you again?"

"You're seeing me now."

He made a face.

"I want to see you for more than half an hour at a time."

He took a bite of my food and I stared at his lips as he ate. His Adam's apple bobbed as he swallowed. "I want a whole night."

I felt my cheeks get hot. He was getting ahead of himself. But was he really? I hadn't said no to anything he had asked of me. He might be a creep, the kind of guy a girl should avoid, but he could also be the perfect person for a stupid girl who didn't know any better to lose her virginity to.

Maybe if I had zero expectations . . . maybe I wouldn't get hurt.

Because it wasn't like Mr. Tattooed Sex God was going to stick around. Even stupid, inexperienced me knew that.

Besides, I didn't think I had the strength to say no. I knew I had to try. To stop this thing that had started between us. It wasn't going to go anywhere, and my brother needed me.

"I don't know what you want."

I felt naked, totally exposed when I lifted my eyes to his.

"You. Just you."

I shook my head and pushed away from the table.

"Look, you're nice and all but . . ."

"Nice?"

"Well, yeah."

He stood up, crossing the tiny kitchen in two steps. He stared down at me, not touching me.

"I'm sorry, Callaway. My life is . . . complicated."

"I can handle it."

"What for? Why even bother?"

His hands came up to cup my chin, tilting my face so I had no choice but to look into his eyes. His thumb brushed my bottom lip and his eyes stared hungrily at my mouth.

"For this."

His mouth crashed down on mine. I realized belatedly that his other kisses had been tame. He'd been holding back.

This need, this hunger inside him, was far bigger than anything I had ever imagined.

This wasn't Romeo and Juliet. This was heat, pure white heat and power blazing between us. I could feel it licking my skin as he pushed me against the kitchen wall and tried to melt into me.

My thigh was hoisted up as he worked his hips into me. Our tongues tangled as he held me firmly in place, grinding his erect cock into me through our clothes. Considering this was more than I'd ever done before, I was more than over whelmed.

I was not ready for this.

I was not ready for *him*.

"Wait."

His hand was sliding under my shirt to tug on my bra strap. I whimpered at the feeling of his warm hand as it closed over my breast. My nipple responded immediately, pushing up into a sharp point. It only intensified the feelings that were spiraling through my body.

Too much. Too fast.

"Wait."

He lifted his head and stared at me, the thick muscle in his jaw ticking.

"You okay?"

I nodded, then shook my head as he started to kiss me again.

"Callaway . . ."

"What?"

"I have to go. My shift."

He swallowed and nodded jerkily.

"Right. Yeah. Your shift."

He was staring at my mouth as he moaned.

"You sure you can't be just a little bit late?"

"No. I can't." I sighed. "And I'm not ready for this. For any of it."

He stepped back, his eyes glued to my face.

"I'm not going to hurt you, Mols."

When had he started calling me that? That was what my brother called me. And . . . my parents. I shrugged as if it didn't matter. That was my defense. *When everything sucks, pretend like you don't care. Then go cry your face off when you're alone.*

"I know, I just . . . I don't really have time to date."

He stepped forward again, pressing me into the wall.

"We'll make time."

I stared up at him, heat swirling in my belly. Then I swallowed.

"You're a really great guy, Callaway."

He narrowed those gorgeous green eyes at me.

"Don't."

"But I'm not looking for anything."

"Don't."

His voice was raw. Ragged. Painfully exposed.

"I'm sorry. I can't see you right now."

He stared at me for a long minute more before turning on his heel and walking away. I flinched when I heard the front door close behind him.

I'd done the responsible thing. The right thing for me and for Tommy.

So why did I feel so wretched?

CHAPTER FIVE

Callaway

"*M*ore."

Donnie leaned backward behind the bar, staring at me like I was a dog on a fucking skateboard. I didn't care. I felt lower than a dog. Hell, at least dogs were loyal. People petted them. Molly would never have told a cute little dog to fuck off.

"What?"

He just shook his head and poured me another shot of tequila. I held out my hand and he grudgingly put the bottle in it. It was the good stuff, not the swill he served everyone else.

I ignored the shot glass and tipped the bottle back, letting it slosh into my mouth. It burned my throat on the way down. Good. I wanted to feel pain. Anything to blot out this crazy feeling inside me.

Because of her.

It was hard to believe, but I'd been rejected. Not just rejected. Cast aside. And by a little girl. A little girl who wanted me.

A little girl who had melted in my arms.

"Molly . . ."

"What did he say? Did he take Molly?"

Lucky leaned down and stared at me, checking my pupils. He'd come up with Whiskey and me, but he'd been out of the country on a tour of duty for the past two years.

"Welcome back, fucker."

He grinned at me, his clean-shaven head gleaming in the neon lights. Donnie clasped his forearm and hugged him over the bar. Jack and Whiskey came in with Dev a few minutes later.

"Well, well, well. Look what the cat dragged in."

Dev was eyeing Lucky, wondering if he was still the crazy young guy who could give even me a run for my money. Lucky saluted Whiskey, which made us all laugh.

"At ease, soldier."

Lucky plucked the bottle out of my hands and took a swig. Then he looked at it, shaking his head.

"How much of this have you had?"

I moaned and reached for the bottle.

"Not enough."

"Hey, man, if you're rolling on Molly, you need to hydrate." He looked around at the rest of the guys, who were staring at him openmouthed. "What? It's true. Ravers die all the time when a fucking bottle of Gatorade could have saved their lives."

"I'm not rolling. But I will take any drugs you have on you."

"Sorry, man. I don't partake anymore."

I sneered at him and did the shot that had been sitting there all this time. I reached blindly for another drink and found a cold bottle of beer pressed into my palm. Around me, my brothers caught up with our old friend. Baby pictures were passed around. Wedding rings were counted. Donnie's cousin Mac took over serving while the rest of them shot the shit.

"We're the only ones left, eh, Callaway?"

I moaned again.

"He said Molly! I fucking heard him!"

Donnie grabbed the bottle of tequila out of Lucky's hand.

"I think he's talking about a girl."

"Only one?"

Jack's voice was so deep, only dogs could hear it. And the guys, apparently. Everyone laughed. I glared at them all.

Some brothers they were. I was heartbroken and they laughed.

"You guys suck. Everybody sucks. Except her."

"She wouldn't suck?" Lucky laughed, slapping my back. "You must be losing your touch, man."

"Wouldn't do anything. Never been with anyone before. She said . . ."

Whiskey leaned in, staring at my face.

"She said what?"

"She said I was a nice guy but she didn't have time."

"You are shitting me."

I shook my head and laid it on the bar, moaning pathetically.

"A woman . . . turned you down?"

"She said you were *nice*?"

Lucky made an 'ooh' sound which made me want to punch him. So I did. But I didn't put my heart into it.

"Ow, fucker." Lucky started grinning like an ape. "Or actually . . . not a fucker."

He found this hilarious. Thankfully, the rest of the guys did not.

Dev cleared his throat.

"Did you say she's a virgin?"

I nodded miserably.

"She put the brakes on. I was right there, man."

"Maybe it's for the best, man. It's kind of a big deal for a girl. You can have five girls a night."

"I don't want five girls!" I said, swinging my arms dramatically. My beer spilled and Jack stepped back to avoid getting splashed. "I just want her!"

"Holy shit." Donnie's voice was awestruck.

Whiskey was grinning.

"I thought this day would never come."

I stared around at the guys and shook my head.

"You guys don't get it. She's perfect. She's so good and I . . ."

"We get it, Cal. We do."

"Get what?"

Everyone turned to look at Lucky. He was the only one with a dumbfounded look on his face. Mac walked over and had the same stupid expression.

"Love, you idiot." Whisky smacked the back of his head for good measure, making Lucky rub his head and glare at us.

"Why does everybody keep hitting me?"

"Because you're an idiot." Jack winked at him to take the sting out. "How long have you known this girl, anyway?"

I cleared my throat.

"Couple of days. How could this be happening to me?"

Jack slapped my back. It was supposed to be brotherly, but since the man was built like a redwood, it felt more like a two by four landing on my shoulder.

"Happened to me in less than five seconds."

"Five? Seriously?"

"I knew that first night."

"No, you didn't." Dev was grinning ear to ear. He loved teasing Jack. He and Donnie were the only ones who could get away with it. "You fought it tooth and nail."

"Yeah, I did. But I knew. I knew it was a lost cause. That's what pissed me off."

"Alright, I'll bite. Is she hot? When can we get a look at her?"

"Lucky, if you even look at her, I will sew your fucking eyeballs shut."

He thought that was hilarious. To soothe my pride, I took another swig of tequila. Then I pulled out my phone. I had taken a couple of pictures of Molly. I showed the guys.

"Is she sleeping? I thought you said you didn't hook up?"

"That's creepy, man." Lucky snickered. "She *is* hot though, stalker."

I shrugged, staring at my phone. Molly looked so pretty curled up on her bed. I hadn't been able to resist. I found another shot of her I'd taken through the glass when I was outside the garden center.

"Here she is at work."

"You followed her to work?"

"Hell, no. I was waiting to pick her up." I sat up straight. "But that's a good idea. I know where she works. I could go there now and—"

"No. No, no, no."

A chorus of nos rang out as heavy hands pushed me back into my seat.

"How about tomorrow? Go and see her tomorrow, okay, champ?"

"Yeah, go tomorrow, stalker." Lucky was snickering again. "Man, how the mighty have fallen. I heard you were the king of dicks around here."

He looked around, waving Mac over.

"This guy has been swimming in it since day one."

Mac grinned. "Yeah, I noticed."

"Callaway, what happened, man? I thought you had your pick of any female in a twenty-mile radius."

Donnie snickered. "More like fifty."

"Yeah, man, just move on."

"No! Who cares about other women? Nothing matters without her."

I leaned my head against the bar again.

"Man, I hope I never sound that pathetic over a chick."

"Shut up, Lucky." Lucky ducked, sensing another slap. Instead, Whiskey rubbed his hands together. "Callaway needs our help. Who's in?"

Everyone except Lucky said yes. I glared at him, bleary-eyed, until he said he was in. I felt marginally better, though I didn't understand how they were going to help me. Even Mac was in, and he was the coldest bastard I'd ever met.

"You said she didn't have time for you, man?"

"Yeah, she works two jobs to help pay for her little brother. He's in the same home as Bonnie."

"A kid?"

I nodded at Dev, who looked concerned. He got like that about kids. All the guys did.

Jack's deep voice boomed out.

"What's wrong with him?"

I shook my head.

"You know what? I don't even fucking know."

CHAPTER SIX

Whiskey

I whistled softly to myself as I pulled into the driveway and looked at the house. It hadn't been much to look at at first, but I'd worked it over to my lady's specifications. It now had white trim and blue shutters, with a black front door. It did look sharp, I had to admit. My Becks had excellent taste.

I smiled.

She had damn good taste in baby daddies to start with. She'd picked me, and I was doing my damn best to make everything perfect for her and our baby, and the baby-to-be, of course.

Starting with the house.

My house.

Our house.

Coming home had a whole new meaning since Becks. Since the baby. This was our place, and we were a family. I was a lucky sonofabitch and I knew it.

I opened the door slowly, careful not to make a peep. Not only was our daughter, Eliza, mostly likely asleep, but my pregnant wife most likely was too. She'd been taking lots of naps lately, which I found adorable. She'd be reading a book and doze off where she was, usually curled up in a chair. Sometimes, she made it to the bed. One time, I'd found her dozing with her head rested on her hands, right there at the kitchen table.

So I was expecting some cute little snoring sounds when I walked in. Maybe a dirty diaper to deal with. But that was it.

I hardly expected the shoe to come flying past me, less than an inch from my head.

I turned to see my beautiful, caring wife holding a shoe in the air, an angry look on her pretty face.

"What in the world?"

"Pig!"

"Becks?" Another shoe came flying toward me and I ducked. "You okay, honey?"

"I'm stuck here, starving, and you didn't even bring me anything!"

I stared at her, blinked, and then started laughing. Our house was full of food. She was talking about something else.

She was talking about ice cream.

My Becks had gone absolutely coocoo for ice cream since the second trimester started.

"Now sweetheart, just hold your horses. I have your ice cream. I just forgot it outside."

I slid my boots back on and hustled out to the bike, where I had stashed a pint of chocolate ice cream for my woman on the way home from the club. I grinned as I hurried back in, taking my boots off again before I set one foot on the carpet.

Becks was adamant about no shoes in the house, and I had to agree. Anyone would, once they though about it. Especially with the little ones underfoot. We already had one baby crawling around and putting every damn thing in her mouth. Plus, it cut down on the need to sweep, mop, and vacuum.

Not to mention, I liked seeing my girl's cute little toes.

My Becks was full of ideas.

She was a dynamo. Even pregnant and sleepy, she did more than most people did in a day. She was in nursing school part-time and I couldn't be prouder. Sure, she was frustrated that it was going to take her twice as long to make it through the program and start working, but I told her it was okay to slow down.

She couldn't handle that class load with a bun in the oven. Soon, we would have two little ones underfoot. It was better to take her time and do things right. By the time she was finished, the kids would be ready for school, part-time at first, but I could handle the drop offs and pick ups. I had it all planned out, I told her. She'd reluctantly agreed to go part-time, and a good thing too, considering how many naps the woman was taking.

"Here you go, sweetheart." I held up the pint and she glared at me. "How about a kiss?"

She narrowed her eyes for a second and then whoosh, there was my pretty girl, smiling at me and offering up those sexy lips for a kiss. I held her tight, her hard belly pressing into me.

"You didn't forget."

"I didn't forget."

I squeezed her bottom and breathed into her ear before biting it.

"You want to thank me now, or later?"

"Later!"

She grabbed the ice cream and swooshed into the kitchen. So much for having a quickie before ice cream. I chuckled as I followed her in, taking off my jacket and grabbing a bottle of water. We filtered our own and used refillable bottles. It wasn't all that hard once you got the hang of it.

My woman was very concerned about the environment, as

well as all of our health. She even had me taking a multivit-amin and skipping meat a couple of days a week! I had to admit, I didn't really mind Meatless Mondays. She made everything fun.

I sat down across from her, watching her dig into her ice cream. She moaned in ecstasy at the first bite. I hadn't worried about keeping it cold. She liked it when it started to go soft.

"Nice and melty, right?"

She nodded happily and took another bite. I knew my woman. I chuckled to myself, pulling off my jacket.

"You're never going to guess what happened."

"What?"

"Never in a million years."

"Omg, what, Whiskey? Tell me already!"

She was getting cranky, even with the chocolate. She was pretty far along, so I cut her a lot of slack. Plus, I thought she was cute when she was cranky.

"Callaway met someone."

Her eyebrows shot up. She stared at me, a spoonful of chocolate ice cream paused in midair.

"Someone?"

"A girl."

"He meets girls all the time."

"No, not a club girl. A civilian."

Her eyes got even wider.

"And?"

"And she blew him off."

"You're joking. I thought Callaway never got turned down."

"He doesn't. He doesn't even have to try. Or ask."

"But this time . . . ?"

"He asked. Apparently, he asked her out on a date."

"Who is this girl? I feel like we should give her a medal. Or a parade."

"Cal said she's real sweet. She works at the nursing home his gran is in. He said . . ."

"What?"

I hesitated a minute and then forged ahead.

"She's a virgin."

"Callaway and a virgin?"

I nodded. My woman sputtered at me. Then she sat back in her chair and started giggling. She held the spoon aloft, the ice cream forgotten for the moment.

"Poor Cal. Oh my goodness, that is too much. How's he taking it?"

"Not good. He's a mess."

"What else? What's she like?"

"He said she's a good girl. She's got a lot on her shoulders."

"And she didn't like all the tats?"

"No. She liked him, tats and all. But she has two jobs and her brother's in the nursing home. She doesn't have time to date."

"Wow. And he's onboard with signing up for all that? Wait!" She gave me a suspicious look. "Does she have fake boobs?"

"I don't think so. She looked very sweet in the photo he showed us."

"Cal took a picture of a girl? On his phone?"

"Yeah. A couple."

"Are you *sure* it wasn't porn? Or a sex doll?"

I laughed and nodded.

"Yes, Becks. It was a candid photo of a real person."

"Jesus, that sounds so mature of him. What's he going to do about it?"

"Right now, he's three sheets to the wind. I don't think he's going to give up though."

"Good. I hope he settles down and has five babies. Then maybe he'll stop trying to corrupt my husband."

"He doesn't try to corrupt me!"

"He doesn't get shitfaced in our garage and try to keep you up all hours?"

I cleared my throat sheepishly. I didn't go out to party anymore so Callaway tried to bring the party to me. He'd even offered to babysit, though he was almost always a little bit drunk as far as anyone could tell. Becky had wisely said no.

"What's this girl's name?"

"Molly something."

She dug her spoon deep into the ice cream. I was pretty sure I heard her scrape the bottom. Good. The sooner she finished, the sooner I could take her to bed. My woman got cranky if I didn't love on her at least once a day.

I got a little cranky too.

"Well, I sure hope Molly doesn't get serenaded tonight. I know what you boys like to do when you're drunk and heartbroken."

I smiled and didn't argue. If she left me again, I'd do more than serenade her. But knocked-up like she was, I didn't have too much to worry about. Becks was mine, and she knew it.

"Come on, sweetheart. I'm taking you to bed."

CHAPTER SEVEN

Callaway

"*U*gh."

I rubbed my face, wondering where the jackhammering was coming from. I realized it was just my head and opened my eyes, staring at the ceiling. I was home, though I had no idea how I'd gotten there. I looked up at my legs, which were somehow above me.

I turned my head and saw the legs of my coffee table beside me. I was on the floor with my legs up on the couch.

Click.

"What?"

I heard snickering as a flash filled the room. Then another. I covered my eyes, flailing with my hands to block the light.

"I need a picture of this shit."

"Lucky, you motherfucker!"

He was above me, snapping pics on his phone. I growled, ready to tear his throat out. Well, metaphorically speaking. I wouldn't actually murder the fucker, tempting as it was.

I *was* going to trash his phone, however.

That's when I realized I was cuddling one of the couch pillows against my chest.

"You look so sweet with your woobie." He chuckled to himself, still snapping pictures. "Or should I say, your *Molly*? You said her name about a thousand times last night."

"That's it!"

I jumped up and threw myself at him, fists flying. He was laughing when my fist connected with his jaw the first time. He stopped laughing when I hit him the second time. And the third time.

He fought me back, and we wrestled, finally breaking apart to lie on the floor a few feet apart. I stared at the ceiling, breathing heavily.

"You hit like a girl."

I started laughing. Lucky was a fucking bastard, but he always made me laugh. I loved the sonofabitch, even though he was a pain in my ass.

"I'm hungover, even for me. You got off easy."

He leaned up on one arm and wiggled his eyebrows at me.

"Oh, I am easy. Ask the ladies you turned down last night. I gave all of them a ride."

I shook my head.

"I hope you wrapped your sausage."

"'Course I did. I'm a Marine."

He saluted me and leaned back against the TV stand. I forced myself to sit up and moaned, grabbing my head.

"Goddamn, why did I drink so much?"

"You were bitching about that girl, remember?"

I did remember. And if I wanted to do something about it, I was going to have to clean up my act.

"I need to shower. Make yourself useful and brew some coffee."

He nodded.

"Two Bloody Marias coming right up."

I shook my head and laughed. He really was a fucker. But he was my fucker.

***

Thirty minutes later, I was riding toward the other side of town. I was clean and looked slightly less hungover. I wanted to check on Molly before I headed to the clubhouse. Most likely, I'd work at the club a few hours if anyone wanted ink and then I'd drink myself into a stupor again.

But I needed to see her first, even if it was just at a distance.

Lucky had gone off to do whatever bastards did during the day. He was starting a job as a contractor next week, but for the moment, he was freewheeling. I was almost *always* freewheeling, though suddenly, that didn't seem like a good thing.

Yeah, I made my own hours. Yeah, I was paid well for my skills with the tattoo gun. Yeah, I was even saving up to buy a house somewhere, hopefully in the woods with lots of room around it.

It was probably weird for a party guy to want a secluded house, but that's what I wanted. What I'd always wanted. A rustic place I could fix up. I pictured cold beers on the porch, maybe a deck of cards or my guitar in my hands.

I hadn't played in forever, and I never played in front of others. I'd never wanted to be a rockstar like every other teenager alive. I just liked doing things with my hands. And I liked music.

I'd let that get away from me, I realized. I hadn't started a project in years, let alone finished one. I used to do things around the house for my granny, but that didn't count.

All I did was drink, party, ride, tat, and fuck.

And now, I wasn't even doing that.

I'd flushed the drugs in my apartment the night I met Molly. I didn't want her to come over and see that shit. Of course, the likelihood of her coming over had taken a nose-dive yesterday when she called things off.

I clenched my jaw and sped up. I wasn't the kind of guy girls blew off. I was the guy they begged for.

And I would really, really love to see Molly beg.

A few minutes later, I was pulling into the parking lot. I assumed she was working the same hours today, though how she was on her feet after weeks of this, I had no idea. I was going to have to insist that she give up one of her jobs . . . or ask them to pay her more and take fewer shifts.

The other solution I'd come up with was even better. I'd have her move in with me so her expenses would be less. Then she'd only have to worry about her brother, and I could help with that too.

Yeah, that was a brilliant idea. Get her to move in. I could say it was just to help with money, but she'd be there, close at hand, sharing a bed with me every single night.

I was practically smiling as I stepped off my bike. I'd talk some sense into her. I'd take good care of her and she'd never want to leave. I'd finally buy that house, and she'd decorate it with her cute little girly things.

Maybe I could even convince her to give me a baby.

I could see it now, my beautiful girl holding a baby to her breast. I could watch her breastfeed for hours. And I would, I decided.

I stalked to the front door and pulled it open, scanning the place for her. There was a bored-looking teenager working one register, then nothing. No one else.

Maybe she'd taken the day off.

Maybe she was at the nursing home.

More likely, she was in the back, taking a break.

I knew she didn't want me interfering, but I had to see her. I'd been out of my mind last night. And now I felt like I was gonna die if I didn't see her. Talk to her. Change her mind.

Kiss her.

I pushed open the door with the big sign on it. The sign I ignored.

EMPLOYEES ONLY

Fuck them. They were asleep at the wheel anyway. The damn store was empty. I'd go wherever the hell I pleased, especially if it meant finding Molly.

I looked around, wondering where to start. It was a big fucking store. I remembered that she sometimes slept in the stock room with the cleaning supplies. She said paper towels made a decent pillow.

There were rows and rows of supplies, some of them reaching to the ceiling. The place was huge, and this part wasn't even open to the public. I walked down a long aisle to the right, my eyes peeled for sleeping angels.

I heard the breathing before I turned the corner. But not sweet little girl breathing. Heavy, creepy ass dude breathing.

A guy was leaning against the shelves, hunched over and staring at something. I squinted at him for a second, then looked past him to see what he was staring at. He was peeking through a hole between the stacks of the boxes. You could just barely see through to the other side.

Molly was curled in the next aisle. I could see the gentle rise and fall of her breathing as her breasts pushed against the thin cotton of her top. He was staring at her through the shelves.

And wanking.

"Motherfucker!"

I roared as I charged forward, knocking the guy onto the floor. He shrieked like a woman as he hit the ground. I heard a soft gasp as Molly woke up in the next aisle. The guy turned over, pushing his junk back into his pants. I stared at him, exhaling actual steam from my nostrils. I wanted to tear him apart.

"What the hell!"

"You motherfucker." I pointed at him, stepping closer. "I'm going to fucking kill you."

His eyes got wide and scared.

"Get out! I'll call the police!" Molly came around the corner, looking like a sleepy angel. He looked at her like she was going to save him. Fucking coward. "Molly, go call 911!"

She looked at him and then at me.

"What are you doing? Go call the police!"

She didn't move. Good girl.

"Get up. I want to knock you down again. This time, with my boot on your windpipe."

He shook his head frantically.

"Callaway, what's going on?"

I glanced at her. The worried look in her pretty blue eyes tore at my heart.

"Later. I need to handle this first."

I gripped the front of his shirt and picked him up, setting him on his feet. Then I held him there while I bloodied up his face.

Bam. Bam-bam-bam.

I tilted my head to the side, deciding. He was still conscious. I figured he had one more hit in him. I wanted him to remember this.

"The SOS takes care of its women."

He paled, fear making him start to blubber.

"You're one of them?"

I nodded.

"If you ever so much as look at her again, I'll cut your fucking dick off and feed it to you."

"Right. Okay. I'll never look at her again."

"What kind of pig does that?"

He was drooling blood on my fist where I held his shirt. I shook him and asked him again.

"What kind of pig are you?"

"A filthy pig. A filthy, disgusting pig."

I smiled at him like all was forgiven. Then I lifted my fist one last time. He stared at my fist, then back at me. He shook his head frantically.

"No. No, no, no, no."

"Yes."

BAM.

He slipped from my fingers and folded onto the ground. I'd even held back, not hitting him half as hard as I wanted to. But he was out.

I checked his pulse and then stood, wiping my bloody hands on my jeans.

"Let's get out of here."

Molly stared at the bloody mess on the floor, then at me. She nodded once.

"I need to get my stuff."

I followed her to the breakroom and waited while she emptied out her locker. She wasn't coming back here again. We both knew that.

I took her hand and walked her out through the back door.

CHAPTER EIGHT

Molly

"You're . . . mad at me?"

Callaway looked shocked. He obviously thought he'd done me a favor by beating the crap out of my supervisor. Well, he was wrong! That had been an easy gig and now it was gone. I had no idea how I was going to dig myself out of the financial hole I was in.

"You cost me my job!"

He stared at me, the muscle in his jaw ticking. How could such a big, strong man be so stupid?

"He was bothering you."

I gritted my teeth. I hadn't said a word on the ride back to my place. I hadn't known what to say. I'd been too stunned by the sudden turn of events.

"No, he wasn't."

"He was watching you sleep with his dick in his hands!"

Ew. Oh, my God. That was disgusting. No wonder Callaway had cleaned the floor with the guy. I tried to bluster through it anyway.

"Yeah, well, I didn't know that!"

"He's a fucking pervert!"

"And you aren't?"

His jaw dropped. I noticed that he had a couple of bruises on his face in addition to the bloody knuckles he'd gotten from beating the crap out of my boss.

"What happened to you, anyway?"

"Lucky. It doesn't matter. I took care of that guy for you. You aren't going back there anyway."

"You were not supposed to come into my work! We agreed on that!"

"I needed to see you!"

"Yeah, well . . ."

I had forgotten what I wanted to say. We stood toe to toe, yelling at each other in my tiny kitchen. He was so worked up his green eyes were practically sparking. I scowled at him and he glared right back at me.

For a second, it seemed like time stood still. Something changed as we stood there, both of us breathing heavily. The tension broke with an almost audible snap in the air.

And then we were kissing. Hot, filthy, messy kisses. Kisses that blew the roof off the other kisses we'd shared. And those had been pretty steamy. Even an inexperienced virgin like me knew that.

He was like an animal, tugging at my clothes while he practically inhaled my mouth. I moaned as his hands gripped my hips, yanking me against his hard body. He pulled my shirt off, then his, never breaking contact for more than a second.

Our bodies crashed together, skin on skin for the very first time. His tats filled my vision when I opened my eyes, quickly shutting them again as he lowered his head to my throat, kissing and biting and sucking my skin.

I heard something crash as he cleared the kitchen table with his forearm, then lifted me on top of it. He unhooked my bra with ease and then pushed me back so that I was half lying on it. His eyes flared as he stared at me, reaching for the top of my jeans and quickly unfastening them.

His big hands moved to his belt buckle. My mouth was dry as I stared at the skin above his jeans. His stomach was flat, with a narrow strip of hair that disappeared into his pants. I realized there was nothing under the worn-in denim. Callaway was buck naked under there.

He didn't shove them down, however.

He was too fixated on me to finish undressing. More specifically, he was fixated on my chest. He moaned as his hands closed over my exposed breasts, my nipples rising up to meet the rough, hot flats of his palms.

"Jesus, Molly."

His voice was raw as he fondled me, not being too rough but not being all that gentle either. Then he bent forward and pulled one of my nipples into his mouth.

Oh, sweet lord in heaven that felt good.

I gasped, my back arching off the table. His hands were busy too. He was stroking my thigh with one hand while his other played with my breast. I moaned as the pressure of his fingers moved to the junction between my legs.

The spot where no one had ever touched me before.

I nearly fell off the table at the feel of it. I'd touched myself there, of course, with varying degrees of success. But this . . . this was a whole other level.

He tore his face away from my breast and stared at me, breathing heavily.

"Molly . . . I have to . . ."

I stared at him as he broke off, gripping my jeans and pulling hard. Cool air hit my sensitive skin, and I realized he'd managed to strip my panties off with my jeans. Just like that, I was naked.

He pulled me up so that I was sitting at the edge of the table and kissed me again. His fingers slid between our bodies and he stroked me again. My worries disappeared with a fresh onslaught of pleasure. I'd never felt lust like this before. I was literally gasping for air.

"I need—"

"It's alright. I know. I'll take care of you, Molly."

His hands moved to undo his belt buckle and I had a moment of clarity. I was about to lose my virginity on a table. With a man I barely knew.

I mean, I *felt* like I knew him through and through, but did I really?

"Wait."

He stopped, his hands on his jeans as he paused. His jeans were slung low on his hips. I swallowed, my throat suddenly feeling *way* too dry.

"I'm not ready for this."

He stared at me, his breathing ragged. I knew this was not what he wanted. But it was too much.

"Please, Mols. Don't shut me out."

"I'm not."

"I need you. I need to be inside you."

"I can't. This is going too fast."

"Okay. We don't have to do that. But let me hold you."

He closed his eyes and slowly pulled his pants back up.

"If you hold me, then we're going to end up having the same conversation in five minutes."

He shook his head.

"No, sweetheart. My pants stay on. Just . . . let me finish you. Please. I need to."

I bit my lip, feeling ridiculous with my bare ass on the old table. It was green Formica from the 1950s and came with the place, but I sort of doubted anything like this had happened on it before.

Even in seventy years.

I finally nodded, and he smiled just a tiny bit. He gripped my thighs and kissed me deeply before pushing me back down on the table. I was breathing heavily, nervous about what was to come. He kissed his way down my body and knelt quickly on the floor.

"Callaway!"

I tried to sit up, but he shook his head, his palm on my stomach holding me down.

"Let me."

He kissed me between my legs, and I was off the table, staring at him like he was a crazy person. But he was smiling.

"Somebody has sensitive skin."

I was naked, standing in the kitchen. I started to cover myself with my hands, and he grabbed me, pulling me close.

"Don't, baby. Don't do that."

He kissed me and I relaxed against him.

"We can go slow. I'll do it another way. Okay?"

I nodded, practically hyperventilating. He stared into my eyes as his fingers moved over my bare skin. The rough pads slid over my bare belly to my pussy. I whimpered a little as he started to toy with me. He eyes held mine as he teased me softly. His touch was so light, it made me want more. More pressure, more friction. More of *him*.

He didn't look away as his fingers started to dance over my clit, circling light and fast on the sensitive nub. He tilted his head to the side, observing me as I started to moan and rock against his hand. He lifted it away, a smug smile on his face as I gasped. Then his hand was back, playing with my folds a bit until he took pity on me and started his rapid thrum again.

Over and over, he did this, each time making me more and more frantic.

"Callaway!"

He smiled at me, licking his fingers.

"Yes?"

"Please!"

"What do you want, baby? You want to come?"

I nodded frantically, letting my head fall back.

"You want me to use my fingers? Or my mouth?"

"Fingers. Oh, God, please."

He shook his head.

"Alright, sweetheart. You asked nicely. I'll give you what you want."

He hoisted one of my legs up around his waist and reached below my thigh to slip a finger inside me. We both moaned.

"You're so tight, baby . . . Jesus."

His other hand found my clit. He used his index finger to press down on it and circle. I gasped at the dual sensations of his one finger sliding in and out of me, the other busy driving me wild on my clit. I lost control of my body, writhing and wiggling against him, flexing my back and holding onto his shoulders for dear life.

"That's it, baby. Reach for it."

Callaway's voice was husky and tender, sending me over the edge. I cried out, my head falling back as I peaked and exploded into a thousand shards of light. I shook all over his busy hands. He didn't stop for a second. He added a second finger, sliding it deeper inside me, circling the other finger so quickly I thought that he must be half machine.

I was floating, cresting and falling without coming all the way down. His lips found my neck as I convulsed against him. He made an appreciative sound, a sound that was one hundred percent self-satisfied male.

Of course, *he* wasn't satisfied, I realized. But I wasn't exactly sure what to do about that.

"You did so good, baby."

"Call . . . that was . . . is that normal?"

He grinned at me.

"Probably not."

"It's never been like that when I . . ."

He bit his lip.

"When you what, sweetheart?"

"When I touched myself before."

He swallowed and closed his eyes.

"Lord, give me strength," he whispered, and I giggled. I reached down his body. He caught my wrist, his eyes snapping open again.

"Can I . . . do that for you?"

"Yes, but not today. I don't think I can handle it."

"Are you sure? I want you to feel good too."

He pressed a kiss to my forehead.

"I do feel good. Now, why don't you take a nap? I'll be back in a few hours to take you to Crestwood."

He picked me up and carried me to my tiny bed. He even pulled the covers back and put me inside. He laughed when I pulled a nightgown out from under my pillow and slid into it.

"What?"

"You're just . . . too cute to be real."

"Well, I am real."

"I know."

He pulled the blankets up and over me.

"You rest. I'll see you later." He held up my keys. "I'll let myself out."

"Okay."

He pressed a kiss to my forehead, and I sank into my pillow with a smile on my face.

CHAPTER NINE

Callaway

"She's going to kill me."

"What did you do now?"

I pulled on a beer and leaned over the piece of wood I was sanding. I'd needed to get into something tonight. And since heavy drugs were off the table, woodworking was the next best thing.

"No, she's not mad. I mean . . . you know."

"She took you back?"

"Yeah."

"But she still won't screw you?"

I gave Whiskey a sour look and he laughed.

"This is unreal. You are the guy who has never *not* gotten laid. What was your record again?"

"Ten."

"You fucked a girl ten times in one night?"

"No. I fucked two girls, five times each. Actually, I think it was four and six."

"And now you're a monk."

"She's worth the wait." I adjusted my nuts, saying a prayer that I wouldn't have to wait too long. My balls were heavy and full. They felt like lead weights. I doubted whacking off would even put a dent in the load I was brewing. "Molly is special."

Whiskey nodded. He might like taking the piss out of me, but he got it. He'd been head over heels with Becky from the start. He'd waited for her too.

I focused on the table I was making. It was a simple side table, but I was using it as a test run for an idea I had for a larger dining room table. I was starting to think about settling down, and this was a step in the right direction.

"You have any hickory around? I want to do an inlay."

"Jack probably does. He has everything."

Whiskey and I were handy, but Jack was a master craftsman. Bikes and woodworking, and probably anything that required dexterity and know-how. I aspired to be as good as him someday. Of course, he couldn't tat like I could. But I wanted to be able to make furniture and build a house like he could.

We'd all been over to help out with his secret project a couple of days a week for months now. If it had still been light out, I would have gone over there now. The big man was teaching me a lot, and I was eager to repay the favor with sweat. Even Lucky and Mac were helping out, though Lucky was a contractor so he probably enjoyed it a whole lot less.

"The table for your place?"

"Yeah. Unless Jack needs it."

"I think Jack has enough furniture."

I nodded. Jack had been building out his industrial building downtown for years, even before he partnered up with Janet. And it was a partnership. They were so tight it was hard to remember a time before they were together. But I'd known Jack back when he was called *The Viking*. The man never smiled back then. Nowadays, it was rare to see him without a smile or a redheaded tot clinging to his enormous frame.

"If things go right, I might be ready to get a bigger place. Been planning to for a while, anyway."

"Yeah?"

"Gran could stay with me if I had a house. If she wanted to. I think she likes the nursing home. But if there were grandkids, I bet she would change her mind or at least come over."

Whiskey yelped as he grabbed his foot. I stared at him. He'd dropped his hammer on it. He put his foot down and stared at me like I was a crazy person.

Of course, most people knew I was a wild man, so that wasn't surprising. Whiskey knew how crazy I could get, more than most.

"What?"

"Grandkids? Who *are* you?"

"You know I love kids."

"Yeah, you're great with Petunia. But I never thought I'd see you settle down."

"I have dreams too, Whiskey."

"Sorry, man. I didn't mean anything."

"You don't have to apologize to me, Whiskey. I was pretty fucking surprised myself."

I went back to my table. I wanted the surface extra-smooth so I could stain and wax it. No polyurethane for me. I was a purist. I hated that shiny shit.

Next, I would cut out some thin slivers and shapes to add a darker wood. It had to be perfect because I wasn't a fan of slathering wood glue all over the place. As soon as I got some other wood, anyway.

It had to be just right.

I hadn't thought about Molly in almost five minutes! I congratulated myself and then realized I was thinking about her again. The way she'd looked in the kitchen. The sweet way she smelled. And the sexy noises she'd made when she came.

I groaned, thinking about how Molly had felt on my fingers. She was so shy, she wouldn't even let me kiss her sweet pussy. She'd nearly collapsed after I finally let her come. I could still taste her from when I'd licked my fingers clean.

She was so sweet. So pure. So goddamn tight. I had a feeling she might squeeze my dick off. I'd been so close to coming in my pants that I practically ran out of there.

Yeah. Me. The man who could stay hard for hours. I'd nearly busted a nut with her barely even touching me. One stroke. Through my pants.

Oh, I was a dead man.

I smiled grimly. I would get her, eventually. I would get her and I would blow her mind. Give her so much pleasure she never wanted to leave. I just had to be patient.

I'd seen a show late one night about training falcons. I watched weird shit when I came home from the clubhouse sometimes, especially when I'd been partying. You didn't force a falcon to do your bidding. It was a seduction. You let the bird get used to you, then you trained it to your hand. You never actually tamed the bird. It was always a wild thing. It was only tame for you.

That's how I had to do this. Not that she was wild, but she was different. She wasn't a girl who'd been with a hundred guys or knew the ropes. She was special. Beyond special.

She was perfect.

I knew Molly would be more than worth the wait. I grimaced and adjusted my aching package. I would tame her to my hand. I just had to live long enough to survive it.

"Speak of the devil."

I smiled without lifting my head. I looked over my shoulder to see Jack pull into Whiskey's driveway. The roar of his ride was unmistakable. We all knew the sound of each others' engines. It was like a fingerprint, but for club guys.

Jack walked in and looked at us. Without a word, he picked up a tool and started working on a half-finished bookshelf Whiskey was building for his little girl's room. A lot of the baby stuff was getting moved into the smallest of the bedrooms for the baby who was on the way.

"Callaway's gone soft, Jack."

Jack grunted. To my ears, it sounded like approval. He didn't preach or dole out advice, but I could tell when he thought I'd gone too far. Which was pretty much all the time lately.

Jack, for one, would be happy if I could get this to work with Molly.

Not as happy as *me*, of course. And definitely not as happy as my aching cock.

"She took me back. Well, kinda."

"She's holding out on him." Whiskey snickered, clearly enjoying having me at a disadvantage. He was getting laid. Everyone was getting laid except me. Lucky had picked up the slack with the club girls since I'd stopped putting out. Even Mac hooked up now and then, though he was pretty fucking quiet.

Again, Jack's chest made a low rumble of approval.

"I need to find her a job. One where nobody is going to paw at her. Or whack off while she's taking a nap."

That might make other guys pause, but Jack just nodded. He made an adjustment to a shelf that wasn't quite fitting and stood up.

"Okay. We'll handle it."

He didn't mean he would take care of it. He meant that *we* would. As a team. We all worked together like pieces of a machine. We were all cogs. Big, fucking scary-looking cogs in

Jack's case. But without each other, we were just individuals. Together, we could move mountains.

I took a swig of my beer and smiled.

It was going to be okay.

We were going to handle it.

CHAPTER TEN

Molly

I pressed a kiss to my brother's forehead, smoothing his hair back. I looked calm outwardly, but inside, I was devastated. I wasn't going to be able to cover the cost of keeping him here. Not even close.

I should have known this wouldn't work. Even with two jobs, I wasn't going to make the monthly cost. But I had hoped I might be able to squeak by. My brother had Medicare, but a fancy place like this required supplemental insurance for a long-term stay.

I was still trying to figure it out, but since I didn't have a laptop, I was doing it all on my phone.

I felt my phone vibrate and pulled it out of my purse. I smiled when I saw who it was. I hardly ever got texts. You needed friends to get texts. You needed a person who gave a crap. It had been a long time since I'd had that.

But I had someone now.

Callaway.

And he was right on time.

I'm outside.

How he knew what time I got off every shift was beyond me. The man was simply there, looking after me. He had been, pretty much from the moment we'd met. I blushed a little, thinking about yesterday afternoon in my kitchen. I was well-rested for the first time in weeks.

But I was also . . . curious.

I was going to lose my virginity to Callaway. It was inevitable. I knew that now. Even if my brain was certain that he would disappear on me one day, my gut was telling me something else. And my heart, well, I wasn't ready to even think about my heart.

I squeezed Tommy's hand and stepped to the window, using the reflection to adjust my clothes and hair. I even put a little lip gloss on. I had never been particularly vain, but having a gorgeous guy around definitely brought out my girlie side. Then I went outside to meet Callaway.

As always, my heart did a little flip-flop when I saw him.

He was so strong, so handsome, and *so* dangerous-looking. He was not a knight in shining armor. But he *was* protective. He'd proven that again and again.

And he certainly knew what he was doing when it came to kissing and . . . other stuff. He must know everything about sex. I blushed again as he pulled me close and kissed me. I sighed, trying not to melt into him. I felt like a girl in a movie. The girl the audience knew had absolutely no chance against the handsome hero.

Or bad guy. He looked more like a bad guy. A sexy, naughty bad guy.

Actually, Callaway was probably a little bit of both.

He finally lifted his head, staring down at me. His gaze was so intense, so hungry, I almost took a step back.

Courage, Molly! Don't be a wuss!

It was Tommy's voice I heard in my head this time. He loved shit-talking me like that. It was probably a rule that little brothers had to do that. I closed my eyes, trying to regain my composure. Then I looked up at Callaway and smiled.

"Where to?"

His green eyes crinkled at the edges.

"I figured I might feed you. Then I have a surprise." He tilted his head to the side. "Unless you want to go right to bed."

My cheeks burned hot and I started stammering. I *did* kind of want to go to bed. But I was also nervous about it.

Really, really nervous.

"I—um, well . . ."

He laughed.

"I meant to sleep." He took my hand and kissed the back of it, rubbing his thumb over my wrist. "But I'm open to anything."

I shook my head at him. He was incorrigible. The man clearly had sex on the brain, but he was so adorable about it that I couldn't be mad.

"Breakfast. Please. And then I have some paperwork to do."

The social worker at the nursing home had printed out some forms for me. She was pretty much a lifesaver. But it was only the first step in getting Tommy on Medicaid. That's what he needed if he was going to stay in the nursing home. Otherwise, it would be another state-run facility, and I didn't want that for him.

Callaway just nodded and helped me onto his bike. Then he climbed on in front, pulled me against his back, and took off.

As always, I couldn't quite believe I was on the back of a

motorcycle. I leaned my cheek against the smooth leather of his jacket, closed my eyes, and let go.

I let go of expectations. I let go of my fears. I let go of all the things that were holding me back.

I just was.

CHAPTER ELEVEN

Callaway

I opened the door, doing my best not to stare at Molly's ass as she walked in. I lost the dare but managed to lift my eyes before she turned around to look up me. The innocent look on her beautiful face nearly brought me to my knees.

I want to defile you. I want to do unspeakably filthy things to you. I want to love you.

I stopped short, shaking my head. *Love?* Where the hell had that come from? I didn't even believe in love. I was a pragmatist. Yeah, I felt protective of Molly. Yeah, she was special and had turned off my 'bang everything that moves' switch. It was instant. I wanted her and her alone.

But love?

The truth was, I already knew that I wanted a future with her, not just sex. But at the moment, it was really hard not to focus on the sex, especially since I wasn't getting any.

Zero sex. Me. It was hard to wrap my head around.

This was a first for me. My dick hadn't been this dry since before puberty. I had been completely celibate since we met. And I was going to stay celibate until she was ready. I fucking hoped it was soon, though, because I felt like my balls were so heavy they were made of rocks. I felt them pulse and turn over just from looking at her.

> *Focus, Callaway. Don't get ahead of yourself. Sex is just the beginning.*

"Where should we sit?"

She was so sweet I almost kissed her. I slid an arm behind her lower back and guided her to a booth. I took the seat facing the door. That way, I'd see a threat before she was in danger. Not that Mae's was dangerous. It was a known SOS hangout. And Mae was officially family to the club. No one would mess around here, but it didn't matter.

My protective instincts were in full effect. I was on high alert.

That was a new thing. I was constantly scanning for bad guys when I was with her. The only other time that had happened was when I was babysitting Eliza the few times I'd been allowed.

And usually, with someone else present. It had taken Becky a while to know I took the responsibility seriously. I didn't blame her. I was a party animal. But I never partied around the kids. That just wasn't right.

But babies. I loved babies. They were so damn cute!

I grinned, imagining Molly's belly all round with my baby tucked safely inside. She would make an amazing mother. And she was so beautiful, I knew our baby would be too.

There you go again, getting ahead of yourself. The girl
hasn't even touched your dick, jackass.

But the image had taken hold. I wanted a baby with her.
As soon as possible. And she had at least *tried* to touch my
dick. That simple touch through the frayed denim had made
my cock leak precum.

Yeah, that touch *through* my jeans. I couldn't imagine what
it would be like to have skin on skin with her. I'd probably
nut in two seconds like a fucking teenage boy or some shit.

My cock got hard at the thought of it. Her tentative
touch. The look of concentration on her flushed face. The
way her lips parted softly, begging me to kiss them.

I adjusted myself and tried to think about nuns. And
puppies. And kittens. Nuns *holding* puppies and kittens.

But kittens made me remember how soft and sweet
Molly's bare little pussy had been. Just like that, I was close
to losing it. I wonder what the clientele of Mae's would do if
I tossed Molly on one of the tables and had my way
with her?

Yeah, it was a good thing I was already sitting down. My
cock was too big and way too fucking hard to hide. I handed
Molly a menu and tried to focus on the food. My eyes kept
straying to the exposed skin of her throat, and a bit lower,
where the top two buttons of her shirt were undone. It wasn't
much skin, but I had a very good imagination. Plus, I'd seen
her yesterday, in all her naked glory.

Her body was perfect. Flawless. And so clearly untouched
it was driving me absolutely fucking insane.

I moaned and looked back down at the menu.

"Are you okay?"

I nodded curtly, not looking at her. I couldn't. I was going
to do something outrageous if I did. Something crazy even
for me.

And I had the very distinct feeling that Molly would not like it if I pounced on her in public.

"Yeah, I'm fine. What do you want, sweetheart?"

"Maybe an omelet?"

I smiled at her, folding my hands on the table.

"What do you want in it?"

She chewed her lip adorably. I sucked in my breath. I wanted to bite that lip. I wanted to bite her *ass*.

Right before I sank my cock into it.

"Tomato and cheese?"

I nodded.

"Sounds good. You want coffee?"

"No, thank you."

I leaned back and waited for the waitress. It was a new girl, one I hadn't met. But I was sure if she worked here, she was a friend to Kaylee, Sally, Becky, and Mae.

When you were waited on by extended family, you always tipped extra-well.

I ordered for us both and leaned forward. I was having a coffee, black. Molly was having water and an omelet. I'd opted for steak and eggs.

I needed my energy for the day. I had plans for the little miss. And not just in the bedroom.

I was trying to be a good guy, but it was really, really hard not to focus on getting her alone. We had other things to do first. Things I hoped she would be glad about.

"How's Tommy doing?"

She took a sip of her water and smiled at me.

"He's moving around a bit more. I think he's going to wake up soon. He does it every couple of months."

"For how long?"

"Just a few minutes, usually."

"Wow. Any idea how to keep him from slipping back?"

She shook her head.

"No. But the last time, he was awake for almost twenty minutes. So maybe . . ."

She shrugged.

"They told me to give up on him, but he's still in there. I can tell. Sometimes, he even squeezes my hand when he hears my voice."

I nodded. It was heartbreaking. And what a burden for such a young girl.

She held up a manila folder.

"If I can get him supplemental insurance or Medicaid, then hopefully, he can stay where he is."

"What's the other option?"

She wrinkled her nose.

"State home. They don't have radios for music and the beds suck. And I've never seen them change him. I think they left him in dirty diapers for a full day a couple of times."

"Jesus."

I took her hand.

"I'll help."

She blushed a little and looked away.

"You don't have to."

"I want to. I can provide moral support."

She giggled and looked away. The food came and we dug in. I was happy to see that she ate well. The girl wasn't shy about food, and she wasn't the sort to starve herself. Plus, I really liked watching her lips as she ate.

I decided then and there that I was going to make sure she ate well, at least three times a day. I grinned to myself. I was looking forward to plumping her up. Not that she wasn't perfect the way she was.

She was almost *too* perfect.

I threw some money on the table without waiting for the bill. Molly protested and then gave up when I wouldn't budge. She'd eventually get used to my taking care of her.

And she was going to *start* getting used to it today.

She held still like a good girl as I put her helmet on. I kissed her softly and helped her climb on. She was such a tiny thing, there was no way she could ride a machine like this by herself.

Maybe I'd get her a smaller ride, like the one Jack had made for Janet. I wanted her to be able to travel in style if I wasn't around.

Of course, I was hoping I would *always* be around. That was the plan, anyway.

"Where to?"

"It's a surprise."

"I really do need to do this paperwork, see if I can afford to keep him there."

"He might be eligible for other federal and state programs too. We can look online together. Later," I added meaningfully.

"I don't have a computer."

I smiled, even though that broke my heart. The kid really did not have a pot to piss in. Well, that was about to change.

"That's okay. I do."

I climbed on in front of her and pulled her tight against me. We were going to Janet's dance studio. Jack had already texted me the go-ahead.

Janet's dance studio was on the other side of town. As luck would have it, she was looking for a full-time receptionist. She might even be hiring an office manager if things worked out. She hadn't promised Molly the job yet, but she had agreed to meet her. And I knew she going to love the little sweetie on the back of my bike.

It was kind of hard not to love an angel like Molly.

Her eyes were wide when I helped her off the back of my ride. She looked up at the dance studio, which was housed in what used to be a five and dime, and then back at me.

"Dancing lessons?"

I smiled.

"My friend Janet is looking for a receptionist. I figured since I cost you the last job, the least I could do was set up an interview."

Her pretty mouth opened in surprise and she stared at me. Then she launched herself into my arms, squeezing me tightly. I could not stop smiling as I squeezed her right back. Nothing had ever felt so right.

"Come on, let me introduce you."

She nodded and waited as I opened the door for her. Janet smiled and waved when she saw us.

"Janet, this is Molly. Molly, this is Janet."

"It's nice to meet you."

Janet's smile was genuine. I sighed in relief. This was off to a good start.

"Molly, I've heard so much about you."

"You have?"

"Apparently, Callaway has a lot of good things to say. The whole club is talking about it."

I glared at her for blowing up my spot, and she laughed at me. Janet was always cheeky. She was worse than the guys when it came to talking smack and could hold her own with anyone, even a burly biker. Molly had turned an adorable shade of pink.

"Oh."

"So, you're looking for work?"

Molly nodded eagerly.

"Do you have a resume?"

"I'm between computers, but I can get it for you if you give me a few days."

"That's okay. Just tell me what you've done."

I stood there, watching Molly with pride. She listed all her jobs and the skills she used at each one. She was young and inexperienced, but she was a hard worker. And she wasn't afraid to speak up for herself. I have to admit I was impressed.

Especially when she rattled off her GPA and the award she'd won in high school. The girl should be in college, I realized with a frown. A girl like her deserved to keep learning, if that's what she wanted.

How could she be, dumbass? Her brother's in a fucking coma and she's his guardian.

Well, things would change now that she was with me. She wouldn't be alone anymore. The weight would come off her pretty shoulders. I'd handle things. I stopped, realizing she might not like that. My Molly was way too independent.

I amended my thought.

I'd help *her* handle things.

Janet had her come behind the front desk. They put their two pretty heads together and started looking at the schedule to set up a few shifts. They would start on a trial basis. I was grinning ear to ear when we left a few minutes later.

Molly took my hand when I tried to put her helmet on. She squeezed it, stopping me. I looked down at her gorgeous face.

Damn, she's almost too pretty to look at! But I'll do my best to get used to it. To get used to her.

"What's wrong?"

"Nothing's wrong. I just . . . I want to thank you."

I gave her a suggestive grin.

"Thank me with a kiss."

She nodded shyly and stepped in, lifting her chin toward me. I was a hell of a lot taller than her, so even on her tiptoes, she couldn't reach my lips.

*Of course, lying down, we wouldn't have that
problem . . .*

Images of the two of us tangled up in bed flooded my head, immediately sending my cock to full attention. With a groan, I caught her against me, kissing her deep and long. Her arms slid around my neck as she kissed me back, not holding back this time.

HONK-HONK

The sound of passing cars brought me back to reality. We were getting some attention from rubberneckers on the busy road. Whoops.

"Let's get out of here."

She turned pink and I knew she got my meaning. I wanted to be alone with her. I wanted to do things to her. Lots of dirty, filthy things.

"Okay."

"Come on, we'll go to my place. I have that computer you were wanting to use."

I helped her onto the back of my ride and climbed on, reminding her to hold tight before I started the engine. I drove a hell of a lot slower with her on the back, that was for damn sure.

I even followed the damn speed limit, something I never did.

My ride was custom and it had an engine that was faster than anything else on the road. Well, other than Jack's ride. But he had done mine, so they might be about equal.

Either way, it went way faster than the speed limit. Something I took advantage of on a daily basis. But not with her precious fanny behind me on the leather seat.

Just thinking about her sweet ass made my cock so hard it hurt. I resisted the urge to speed home so I could get some relief. Or at least *try* to get some relief.

Soon enough, Callaway.

I fuckin' hoped so, anyway. There was every chance that today would end with my balls turning blue again. I didn't care. I just wanted to touch her. Make her come. It was nuts, but it was the truth.

I just wanted *her*. It was a new sensation for me. My own selfish desires were secondary. Yeah, I knew I would go off like a rocket when the moment came. But all the other stuff that came before the finale had me grinning with anticipation.

Molly's first time had to be perfect, whether it was today or some other time. Hopefully, not in the distant future.

Definitely with *me*.

I pulled into my parking spot in front of my apartment building. The landlady, Mrs. Keeley, loved me and had given me a reserved spot. It was safer under the street light, though nobody in this town would dare touch an SOS bike.

Not unless they were suicidal. It could happen, I guess. Death by biker. It kind of had a ring to it.

"This is where you live?"

I nodded, helping her off the back of the bike.

"Yeah, I've been here since high school. But I'm saving up for a little place. Maybe outside town, where it's green."

"That sounds . . . really nice."

Her eyes were a little starry-eyed. I could tell I'd impressed her. Good. I needed all the help I could get in that department. I decided not to scare her by telling her that I kept picturing *her* living in the house with me.

"Come on, let's get you set up on the computer. I can make us lunch in a little bit."

"Okay. Thanks, Callaway."

I took her hand and squeezed.

"Don't think twice. What's mine is yours."

I held the door open for her and then pushed the elevator button. I usually took the stairs to my third-floor apartment, but today, I had other things on my mind. Like what to do with Miss Molly in a confined space.

The moment the elevator doors closed behind us, I pounced. I pulled her against me, grinning wolfishly. She let out a little surprised squeak as my lips came crashing down on hers. I kissed the hell out of her, using all of my experience to knock her socks off.

It worked.

A soft ding announced that the doors had opened when I finally stopped kissing her. She was pressed against the faux-wood paneling of the elevator, one leg lifted and wrapped around me.

She looked stunned as I grinned at her.

"After you."

CHAPTER TWELVE

Molly

*C*allaway's apartment was . . . unexpected. Sunny and clean, with some pretty cool retro furniture and family photos. It didn't look like the drug-filled pussy palace I had been half expecting in the back on my mind.

There was only thing I didn't like, and it took me a minute to figure out what it was. The apartment was freezing.

I wrapped my arms around me.

"Shit. Are you cold?"

I nodded, and he raced to turn off the AC in a room I couldn't see. He appeared a moment later, looking sheepish. He opened the window and took off his jacket, offering it to me.

"Sorry. I sleep better with the AC on. I must have forgotten to turn it off."

"It's okay."

His leather jacket was deliciously warm and heavy as he slid it over my shoulders. It smelled good too. Like old leather, a hint of cologne, and something else. Something manly but hard to describe.

Not BO, that was for sure.

Callaway *never* smelled bad, from what I could tell. I eyed his hair as he stood there, looking serious. His hair was perfect. Always. The sides were shaved with a styled mop on the top. He was more stylish than your average biker, and that was before you even noticed the piercings and tats.

Never mind that his clothes fit him like a glove and looked well-made and expensive but perfectly worn-in.

"You look good in my jacket."

I could tell he wanted to kiss me, but he didn't. I exhaled, realizing I'd been holding my breath. The kiss in the elevator had overwhelmed me and left me feeling restless and unsettled.

"So, ah, the computer is in the bedroom. Let me get it and bring it out here."

I knew he wanted me to tell him not to bother. That it was fine and that we could work in the bedroom. But I didn't. I was still feeling shy around him and nervous about what he might expect.

And I just wasn't ready to see this big, raw, sexy man's bed just yet.

I was insanely curious about his bed and what might happen in it, but I was equally nervous. Knowing he wanted to take me in there and do all kinds of things with me only made me antsier. I swear I could feel my clothes on my skin, and the tiny hairs all over my body stood up.

And that was *before* I remembered exactly what had happened on *my* kitchen table.

Callaway chose that moment to walk in and caught me staring at the small table that sat just under the window that dominated the living room. He gave me a wry smile and walked over to it, setting down his laptop.

He sat down and looked at me.

"Sit down, Molly." He lifted an eyebrow. "I'm not going to bite."

I sat down next to him and watched as he logged into his Wi-Fi. I stifled a giggle, though it was hard to resist teasing him.

"Your Wi-Fi name is . . . *Mee-maw*?"

He looked mildly embarrassed, which made my heart melt.

"That's what I used to call Bonnie. When I first went to live with her."

I felt questions tumble to my lips, wanting to explode. What had happened to his parents? How old had he been? Had he been scared?

But I didn't say anything. My hands slid under my thighs in a familiar gesture. I always sat on my fingertips when I was unsure of myself, which was a pretty frequent occurrence. Especially around someone so confident and appealing.

"I thought you called her 'Nana'," I mumbled instead.

"Oh, yeah. I used both back then but 'Nana' stuck, I guess."

He slid the laptop over to me and sat back.

"Have at it."

"Thanks."

I leaned forward, and he immediately moved his chair closer, his hand sliding under the jacket to stroke my back. I almost purred in pleasure. His big hand was so warm. The apartment was losing the chill with the warm air coming through the window, but Callaway's heat was different.

Deeper.

Better.

It seemed to penetrate my skin, heating the bones and muscles beneath. I felt like a cat, leaning into someone's hand. His touch was so reassuring I nearly cried.

"What are we looking for?"

"I need to make sure his benefits are still up to date. And

I want to apply for more aid." I stared at the screen. "This is great. I can do all of this online instead of mailing in forms."

"Cool."

He sat there in complete silence while I updated my contact info and checked on the status of Tommy's benefits. No pressure. No distractions. Only his calm presence and patience as I did what I had to do. It took almost an hour, but he didn't make a peep other than to offer me a glass of water.

Finally, I sat back, rubbing the bridge between my eyes.

"Headache?"

"No, I just . . . I think I need glasses. I had a pair but I lost them. It's not a big deal."

"Hell yes, it is." He grinned at me. "I think you'd look cute in glasses."

I laughed, shaking my head. He even made glasses sound like a come-on. Did this guy have any turn-offs?

I asked him and his smile faded.

"Not when it comes to you."

"Callaway."

He leaned in. I could have pulled away but I didn't.

His lips were so soft as they pressed into mine. Warm. Firm. The kiss was tender at first, but it quickly became demanding. His mouth opened, and my lips did the same. His tongue danced into my mouth, and I mimicked his moves, making him growl his approval.

"Couch."

Before I could even react, he'd lifted me off my feet so I was pressed against his body. I gasped at the feeling of his hardness. I could feel his blazing-hot cock through his jeans and my clothes. It triggered something deep inside me, and I whimpered, not recognizing the feminine sound of my own voice.

Then I was horizontal. Callaway loomed above me for a

split second before he came crashing down on me. We moaned in unison as the full length of our bodies made contact. My thighs opened without conscious thought, and he was wedging his narrow hips between them.

"Molly . . ."

His lips found the sensitive spots on my throat. He kissed and licked and tickled me as his hands wandered up and down my body at will. He pulled my earlobe into his hot mouth and tongued it. He was revving me up. I wondered if he knew how far. I was nearly out of my mind by the time he undid the buttons of my shirt and spread it wide.

"Hmm . . . I want you so badly."

I took a deep breath.

"I want . . . you too."

His eyes were hooded and somehow penetrating. It was like he was looking straight through me. But I could see he was struggling with his control.

"But you're not sure how much."

"No. That's not it."

"Okay, not how much." He kissed me. "But how far."

I nodded, nearly forgetting what we were talking about.

"Tell me, Molls."

"Well, maybe a little bit farther . . ."

"But not far enough to go into my bedroom."

"Right. I mean, if that's okay."

"Fuck, Molly. I'm not going to turn down having you in my arms."

He groaned as our lips met again. His kisses were more controlled now, but I could feel the wildness underneath. He *was* a wild man. But he was gentle with me.

I trusted him, I realized with a start.

So I didn't hold back. I felt myself letting go of all my worries, just like I did the first time I rode on the back of his bike. I felt the weight of the world lift off my shoulders.

I didn't hesitate or worry. I wasn't coy. I didn't even think about the big V hovering above us.

Not when he kissed me. Not when he deftly removed my shirt and jeans and bra. Not when he pulled my nipples into his mouth one by one, slathering them with reverent kisses. Not when he pressed a kiss into the white cotton of my panties. When he stared up at me, his eyes were raw with need.

I nodded, even though I felt shy about what he was doing. And I still wasn't ready for what came after.

He didn't speak again. He got to work on me like a starving man at a buffet. My panties disappeared so fast it felt like they dissolved into thin air. The air wasn't as cold anymore, but it felt cool against my most sensitive bare skin.

But not for long. His lips were there too quickly for me to even catch a breath, kissing me and stroking me with his calloused hands.

"Oh!"

His tongue slid up and down the line where my lips met. It was only the second time anyone had ever done it to me, and it was overwhelming. Last time, I had stopped him so fast. Now, I was wondering why I'd been so stupid. I didn't know anything could feel this good. His breath fanned my bare pussy and I nearly flew off the couch.

"Mmm . . . you taste delicious."

The sarcastic part of me wanted to ask 'really?' but I never got a chance. He was too busy proving to me that he really did find me delicious. He licked me like he was licking a bowl for the last of the ice cream. My fingers wound their way into his hair without my noticing. I tugged at it, arching my back and gasping for air.

He added a finger to the mix, rubbing it gently against my clit. I couldn't imagine anything feeling better. Until he switched and pulled my clit into his mouth. Then he strummed his tongue against me. Hard.

I felt his finger slide inside me as the first orgasm hit. I arched off the couch, nearly falling off. For the first time, I wished for a bed. I was ready to float back down to reality but Callaway had other ideas. He leaned back to look at me. I was out of breath and fuzzy around the edges. My eyes focused as he leaned in and blew cool air against my sensitive flesh.

"I'm not finished with you yet," he murmured with a wicked grin.

That was it. I was wide awake. I stared in fascination as he stuck his tongue out slowly and dragged the tip up my pussy. I nearly screamed with pleasure.

This time, he didn't let me come right away. He teased me endlessly, keeping me on the brink. I whimpered in frustration as he paused and stroked my nipples and winked. I wanted to slap that knowing smirk off his face. But not as badly as I wanted to shove his head back between my thighs.

Actually, I want more.

I froze, realizing I was thinking about him. His body. Inside mine. I wanted to do it. The big it. The 'it' that I had resisted for so long.

"Sweetheart?"

Callaway's expression let me know he was thinking exactly what I was thinking.

I shook my head. It was too soon. We were on a couch. I hadn't even seen him without his clothes yet. He moaned in disappointment and gave me a quick smile to let me know he wasn't mad.

"But . . ."

His eyes swept to mine, looking hopeful.

"Maybe we could do this . . . some more? And I could do it, you know, to you?"

He shut his eyes and grimaced.

"Oh, God. Yes. Okay. Yes." He looked at me, and I saw the crazy look in his eyes. He was worked up and trying to play like he wasn't. He looked like he was on the edge of sanity. "But maybe we could go into my bedroom."

I looked toward the hallway, then back at Callaway. I gave him a tiny nod. I wanted more. Just not . . . everything. But close.

And soon.

If I kept seeing him, it was a done deal. And I doubted I could stop this now, even if I wanted to. Sure, I was worried that a guy like him would hurt me. I was sure he wasn't a one-woman guy. But maybe, just maybe, he wanted to be.

I stood up and let him lead me into the bedroom.

CHAPTER THIRTEEN

Callaway

"*O*h, my GOD!"

I gritted my teeth, holding back moans. We were on my king-sized bed, spread out. I'd already had her thighs wide as I ate her sweet pussy again, making her come a third time while my cock pulsed relentlessly in my jeans. Now I was the one who was getting worked over. And I was close to finishing.

Too close.

The sad part was, Molly had barely even begun.

She'd unbuttoned my jeans, smiling shyly up at me. I'd nearly spilled my seed right there and then. Just the butterfly touch of her delicate fingers through the worn denim had come close to undoing me.

It was an embarrassment but there was no hope for it. The woman had some sort of magical power over me. And my cock. Dear God, my cock loved her.

My jeans were on the floor. Sliding them down had released the snake. He was a python around her and ready to strike. She'd stared in shock as my cock literally bounced out of my jeans and bobbed there, pointing up toward my chest.

Her fingertips had felt like fucking rose petals as they trailed curiously over my shaft. Then she'd gotten on her knees and shimmied my jeans down, and her hair had water-falled over my dick. The silky feeling of it was the most exquisite torture I could imagine.

Her fucking hair had almost made me come.

I was in deep trouble and I didn't even care. This one small girl had so much power over me. I should be fucking terrified. But I wasn't. I was in too deep to even know I was at risk of drowning.

Now Molly was climbing back up my body, her gorgeous skin gleaming in the faint sunlight coming in around the edges of the blinds. I wanted to pull the damn blinds open so I could see her. I wanted all the lights on. Hell, I wanted a fucking spotlight so I could look at her in perfect, clear, bright light.

Yeah, that's what I wanted.

But this was a pretty good runner-up.

"Molly . . ."

Her lips were puckered, getting closer and closer to my cock. A shiny drop of precum waited for her. I held my breath as her lips got closer and closer . . . I moaned in ecstasy at the first tentative touch of her puffy lips on the tip of my cock.

She kissed it, then looked up at me, sliding her tongue over the tip. Her eyes widened in surprise.

"It's salty."

The reminder of her innocence made my hips jerk. This wasn't just the best blowjob I'd ever gotten, which it was, even if it ended right now. It was the first she'd ever given.

And she was giving it to me.

I was the luckiest sonofabitch in the whole fucking world.

My balls twisted as she gripped my shaft and lowered her lips to my tip again. She might be inexperienced, but she had paid attention. She was using the moves I'd used on her, and the effect was fucking devastating. I clenched my fists and jaw in an attempt to control what was happening.

It didn't work.

"Molly. Christ! I'm going to come."

She looked up at me but didn't stop. She wasn't taking me very far into her mouth and she wasn't using the relentless rhythm I used when fucking or jacking myself off. Her touch was sweet and gentle and a little erratic. It should not have made me come like a fucking freight train.

But it did.

Oh, lordy, it did.

"Ahh!" I screamed like a fucking banshee as the seed barreled up my shaft and out into her warm mouth. She jerked back and it hit her cheek. I should have grabbed my johnson and angled it away from her. That would have been the gentlemanly thing to do. But she was too fast.

God bless her, she opened her mouth and put it back on my cock. She pulled me into her mouth, making me come even harder.

And then she did something that made it all so much better.

She swallowed.

I kept coming, making grunting sounds like an animal. I had no control over it. Her soft lips held my cockhead in her mouth, and I felt her tongue swirl over the tip as she sucked on me.

It was almost like she wanted to taste my come. She was thirsty for it. And God help me, I couldn't stop giving it to her. I had never come this hard or this long in my life. Not even close. That was saying something, considering how much I'd fucked and how many weird ass things I'd tried. But all that was washed away by this one fucking flawlessly beautiful girl and her first three-minute blowjob.

Jesus fucking Christ. I'm still coming.

"Molly . . . Christ!"

Finally, I gently pushed her away, cursing and moaning as my shaft spurted out the last few drops. I stared at her and at my stomach. We were both covered in milky-white goo. It was a lot, and it wasn't even all of it. She'd swallowed most of it. Just that thought made my dick twitch.

"Jesus, Molly. Are you okay?"

"Of course I am. Did I do it right?"

She smiled at me, looking like a goddamn angel. There was a drop of come on her lip and I moaned. My cock had been there. She'd taken me in her mouth and driven me absolutely insane with the best first-time BJ in the history of the damn world.

And just like that, I was hard again.

Not just hard.

I was in love.

I'd known I was falling. How could I not? She was so sweet, so different from anyone I'd ever known. But right now? It was real. It was one hundred fucking percent happening. I was hers, and I would be for the rest of my natural-born life.

"Molly. Yes, you did it right." I scrambled out of the bed, pulling on my jeans. "Let me get you . . ."

I grabbed a washcloth and let warm water run over it. Then I brought it back to the bed and gently wiped her face clean. I was ready to go again, but I didn't want her to know that. I took the washcloth back into the bathroom and stared at myself in the mirror.

You are fucked, my man. Well and truly fucked.

I smiled grimly, not giving a good goddamn that I was

doomed. At least I'd go smiling. I was pretty sure I was already in Heaven, though what I'd done to deserve it was beyond me.

I cleaned off my stomach and went back into the bedroom. Molly was reaching for my T-shirt. I nearly cried as the soft cotton slipped over her head, covering up her lush curves.

I jumped on the bed and tackled her, rolling her until I was on top. Still trying to control my damn cock. I didn't want to scare her off. Or worse, have her put more clothes on.

"You are amazing, do you know that?"

She caught her lip between her teeth and looked up at me.

"You aren't disappointed? That we didn't . . . you know."

"Are you kidding me? That was incredible. Phenomenal." I kissed her between each word, getting her lips and neck and ears. "I've never felt this good in my life."

"Oh."

Her cheeks were pink as she lay there, looking so fresh-faced and sweet it nearly killed me.

"That's all you can say?" I teased.

"I know you've been with a lot of girls, Callaway. Experienced girls. You don't have to lie."

I gripped her head gently, forcing her to look at me.

"I'm not lying. When you touch me . . . I don't understand it, but—"

I caught myself. I did. I was so close to saying it out loud. Three little words. The same three words I'd never said to another woman, other than my Gran.

It hung there, unsaid, in the back of my mouth. The words wanted to come out. But I stopped them, even though it felt like I was choking on them.

I kissed her again and sighed. I wanted more but I wasn't getting that vibe from her. I brushed her dark, silky hair away from her face.

"You want to use the computer? Eat? Go for a ride?" She looked scandalized when I jerked my head toward the headboard. "Or go for round two?"

"Callaway! You are crazy!"

I nodded.

"Yeah, I am. I'm fucking crazy about you."

There. That was close to the truth, even if it barely scratched the surface. No need to scare the girl. Or worse, scare her *away*.

"So. Hungry?"

She nodded and sat up. I sighed, rolling away. I was more than happy to feed her or anything else she needed. As long as she didn't leave.

I pretty much wanted the girl by my side, all the time.

Fuck.

I watched her put her clothes on, enjoying every second I got to see bare flesh. My cock was still throbbing but I ignored it. The girl had gone way farther than she'd ever gone before, and she'd given me way more than I expected. My cock was going to have to wait for a second go and I knew it.

My shirt came off, and I stared at her slender back as she gathered her clothes from the living room and put them on. A soft ringing made Molly scramble for her purse. I realized she didn't get a lot of phone calls. She hadn't lived in town long, but I didn't think that was it.

She held people at arm's length. She'd had to. She had her brother to worry about, and the two of them were pretty much on their own.

Well, not anymore. She had me now.

Her voice was soft, and I was too busy looking at her to pay attention to what she was saying. I realized something was wrong the moment she put the phone down and turned to stare at me.

"Can you take me back to the home? We have to hurry."

"What is it? What's wrong, Molls?"

She took a deep breath and exhaled.

"My brother is awake."

CHAPTER FOURTEEN

Kaylie

"*I*t's no-VOC, right?"

Dev held up the can of paint proudly.

"Yeah, babe. This is the least-toxic stuff they have."

I nodded, exhaling in relief. Ever since that little line first turned blue, I'd been worrying. Not nonstop, and I refused to give into it, but yeah. I was a worrier.

I was already in full-on mama mode. It sometimes felt like I had been since the moment we'd stopped using protection. I'd started taking prenatal vitamins a week before we even tried. It had come pretty quickly, which was not especially surprising considering how hard Dev had tried.

I blushed. He hadn't stopped trying even after we got pregnant! He'd used it as an excuse to have as much sex as humanly possible. He hadn't slowed down much either.

He rolled up the sleeves of his shirt and winked at me before bending to open the paint can. The look of heat in his eyes was unmistakable. He wanted to be alone and spend some time rolling around on the bed.

My man was insatiable.

My dirty thoughts were interrupted by the sound of

something heavy dropping in the hallway, followed by muffled curses and shushing. I giggled as Dev rolled his eyes.

"In here, guys."

Lucky and Mac stuck their heads in the door. I figured Lucky had been the one cursing, and Mac had shushed him. Mac was quiet and reserved. He didn't give much away. In fact, he often looked like he was made of stone.

It was funny. Even though he was Donnie's cousin, he reminded me more of Jack. Jack was like a giant tree in the forest, looking over everyone, and Mac was like a stone mountain, with his eyes on everything all at once.

Lucky, on the other hand, was a fist full of dynamite. The man was as brash and brazen as they came. And he was second only to Callaway in terms of his crazy antics.

Well, the old Callaway. The new Callaway was something you had to see to believe.

They nodded to me in greeting, respectful as always.

I shook my head at the grin Lucky gave me as I hoisted myself out of the rocking chair. It was my mom's. She'd nursed me in it, and I was going to nurse our child in it. It wasn't anything fancy, just plain brown wood. But Mac was going to paint some small flowers on it as well as a matching mural on the wall, once it was painted. He wasn't a professional, like Callaway, but he was very artistic, especially for a biker.

"Can I bring you guys some iced tea?"

They nodded, and I scooted, heading to the kitchen. I was busy in the kitchen when I heard a noise. I squealed as two arms slid around me and a hot mouth pressed kisses to my neck.

"Dev!"

"Who else were you expecting?"

"You're going to get paint on me!"

I turned around to see him grinning. His hands were in the air.

"Haven't started yet."

I scowled at him another minute just so he knew I was cross with him. I hated being surprised! He knew that! And yet the man loved nothing better than a sneak attack, usually involving kisses or grabbing a particular body part.

He grabbed my bottom now, pressing himself into me and kissing me deeply.

"Dev! We have company!"

"No, we have workers. I was thinking . . ."

I knew what he was thinking, and there was no way I was going into the bedroom with him to fool around with other people in the house.

"No! Absolutely not! You are out of your mind."

He sighed.

"Babe. I need you."

"You had me this morning! Not to mention two times last night."

He looked crestfallen. Absolutely gutted. I frowned.

"The doctor said this was the last week . . ."

"Oh, so that's it." I poked his chest. "You're afraid you're not going to be getting any."

"Babe. It's not quantity, it's quality. I just know I'll miss your . . . qualities."

He tilted his head, trying to see down my shirt.

"You are impossible! The doctor said nothing vigorous in the last month. He didn't say we couldn't do . . . other things."

"Other things?"

Devlin looked like a kid on Christmas morning. I cleared my throat primly and nodded.

"Yes. Other things."

He looked suspicious. "Like what?"

"Use your imagination!" I huffed.

"Lots of other things?"

I raised an eyebrow, trying to control my embarrassment. I shrugged, feeling very shy all of a sudden.

"Yes."

He picked me up and kissed me, his face looking far less worried. He set me down carefully, pressing a kiss to my cheek.

"I look forward to all these other things you're talking about, you wicked woman."

He winked and picked up the cups and pitcher of ice tea. I stared after him, having trouble keeping my eyes off his cute ass. He really did have a perfect bottom. Then I realized what he'd said and threw a dishtowel at his back.

"Wicked!"

He didn't answer. He just started whistling. In fact, he was whistling the whole rest of the day.

CHAPTER FIFTEEN

Molly

Three days.

My brother had been awake for three days.

It was unexpected. A miracle. A miracle I was terrified was about to end.

He'd only had minutes of consciousness in the years following the accident. Snatched moments of clarity, usually months and months apart. But now . . . he'd been with me for three days.

And I hadn't so much as left his side for any of it.

Tommy smiled at me and waved, taking a sip from the juice box in his hands. He'd barely been a teen when all this happened to him. And now he was a young man, seventeen years old. But in his mind, he was still at thirteen-year-old boy.

My heart broke for all the things he'd missed.

Sports. School. Friends. Prom.

Come to think of it, we'd both missed prom.

But he was awake now, and I was determined to keep him

awake. Even if it meant sitting by his side and poking him every time he dozed off.

Which the nurse had specifically told me *not* to do.

I was restraining myself, but it was hard. To say I was anxious was an understatement. He'd slept a few times since he woke up. Each time, I sat there, staring at him, sure he had slipped away again. But he hadn't. He'd only been sleeping.

I dozed a bit in my chair by the window. I'd barely eaten and had gotten zero sleep. I'd only had what Callaway had brought me to eat, diner food from Mae's. Lots of it. I'd shared with Tommy, who had been over the moon about the milkshake. Once Callaway found out that he liked strawberry, a shake had shown up each and every afternoon.

He never came inside though. He'd text me and we'd meet in the hallway. He didn't want to intrude, but he wanted to be there for me. His support was more than I ever could have imagined. He was being amazing. Almost *too* good.

Which made what I had to do even harder.

He was coming now. We were going to talk. I paced back and forth while a nurse came to take Tommy to physical therapy. He had to learn to walk again. His body had been healthy since the accident, other than some bruises and cracked ribs. It had been his brain that took the biggest knock and caused the biggest worry. So I knew he would learn to walk again, even if it took him a long time. I closed my eyes, realizing he could never make it up the stairs to my tiny apartment. We would have to move. Again.

But it was worth it. I would do anything for my brother. Literally anything.

He was awake.

It was a miracle.

"Hey."

I glanced at Callaway, standing in the open doorway. I was

afraid to look at him. Afraid I'd change my mind when I saw his handsome face. He'd been a rock through this. And now I was going to hurt him.

I was about to hurt myself, too.

I forced myself to look at him. The soulful look in his eyes took my breath away. I wished for the hundredth time that I could make this work.

But Tommy was awake. He needed me. He had always needed me, but now he needed me hands-on. And I owed him all the time I had.

Because I knew, without being told, that there was a chance he might fall asleep again and not wake up.

So I was going to give him every single second I had.

I exhaled and straightened my spine.

"How are you doing, sweetheart?"

Callaway came close, pulling me into his arms. I felt his lips press against my hair and nearly cried. He felt so good. He smelled even better.

I shook my head and pushed away from him. I tried to gather my wits, get some semblance of control over myself and my runaway emotions, and get control over the situation. I finally looked at him, and I could tell he knew something was wrong when I looked into his beautiful green eyes. It was right there, raw and impossible to ignore.

"I'm really sorry, Callaway. But I can't do this."

"It's a lot to handle. But you'll get through it. I'll help you."

"No, I mean this. I can't ask you to . . . to do what needs to be done. This is going to be a full-time job."

The muscle in his jaw ticked.

"That's okay. We can handle it."

"I have to focus on my brother right now."

"Of course. I'm here if you need me." He squeezed my hand. "For whatever you need."

I shook my head. It was asking too much.

"Callaway—"

"Don't. I'm not going anywhere." His big eyes were full of pain. "Just don't push me away."

I sighed and walked over to the window. I stared out, not even registering the beautiful sunny day.

"He's going to take all of my time, Cal."

"I know." I felt him come up behind me. "But not forever."

"I don't know what the future is gonna look like. I can't ask you to wait."

"You can."

"No, I've already asked you to wait for . . . you know. You have your own life to live."

"I don't. I don't have a life without you."

His hand slid under my hair to stroke my back. I sighed in pleasure, resisting the urge to lean back against him.

"Don't be ridiculous. Of course you have a life. You had one before we met. You can go back to that."

"You're wrong. I can't go back to that. I won't."

I looked at him and my heart sank.

He looked bad. Really hurt and upset. Damn it. I hadn't wanted to hurt him. I'd imagined his moving on with a hundred girls and forgetting all about me. I was sure they were lining up in droves.

"Molly. We're together now. We are a team. Don't break up the team because you're tired and stressed."

"I don't know. I don't want to, but I can't even imagine how this is going to work."

"It'll work."

"Callaway. I have to find someplace else to live. I already had to tell Janet I couldn't work for her anymore. I owe this place some crazy number. I'm pretty sure it's over ten thousand dollars already. They basically own me. I have no idea how I'm going to support the two of us and—"

He pulled me into his arms again. I let him. It felt so good there. So safe. But I knew I couldn't stay.

"Shh. It's okay. It sounds like a lot of money but it's not. I can pay it."

"I can't let you do that."

"Why not? I love you, Molly. I want to be with you."

I forgot to breathe. He kept stroking my back, murmuring soft words of encouragement. That everything would be okay. That he would take care of me. That he would take care of Tommy.

He said he loved me .

"Callaway, he's going to need so much help. I called my Aunt. She said we could come stay with her in Florida."

"Florida?" He squeezed me hard. "No."

I pulled back and stared at him.

"No?"

"That's right. I said no."

The look in his eyes was unfamiliar. Steely. Hard.

"You can't tell me no. I don't belong to you."

He smiled. It was not a friendly smile.

"Oh, but that's where you're wrong. You do belong to me. And I belong to you, too. That's what being together means. And we belong together, sweetheart. I'm keeping you."

My mouth dropped open. Callaway was talking crazy. It was kind of a sweet crazy, but crazy all the same.

"We just met! You don't own me!"

His smile got wider.

"Oh, I think I do." He leaned in to whisper in my ear. "And I think you know it's true."

I just stared at him.

"You are not moving to Florida. You're moving in with me."

"With you? In your apartment?"

"For now. I was going to tell you but I thought I'd wait until you were less skittish."

"Tell me what?"

"About the house."

"What house?"

"The house I'm buying you."

"What are you talking about?"

He was starting to scare me.

"I was planning to buy a house or build one. I've been watching the MLS. I found a few good options last week. I even went to look at them. I haven't found the perfect place, but I will soon."

"Buying a . . . house?"

"Yeah. It was supposed to be for us. But there's plenty of room for Tommy." He stepped forward until our bodies were touching. "And anyone else who might come along."

"Huh? Who else might . . . come along?"

My brain wasn't working clearly. None of this made sense. Callaway rode a motorcycle. He was in a gang. He wanted to move in with me? I hadn't even given up my V-card yet!

"Babies."

"Babies?"

I just kept repeating what he said like an idiot. It took a second. He held my hips and smiled at me, waiting for the idea to sink in.

"Are you out of your mind?"

He smiled wider.

"Yes. I am."

I spun as the nurse wheeled Tommy back in. I guess he was meeting Callaway now. I was so tired I could barely see straight.

"Hey, man. I'm Callaway. I'm with Molly."

"Cool. You're the one who brought the milkshakes, right?"

"That's me." Callaway stuck out his hand. He was surprising me right now in a really good way. He was cool as a cucumber with my brother. So many people didn't know how to act around sick people. Especially people in wheelchairs. They just stared and acted awkward. Callaway was just being a guy, talking to my little brother man to man.

Tommy didn't miss a beat. He shook hands with Callaway, obviously impressed. I looked at the nurse, Maggie. She was one of the nicer people on staff.

"How did he do?"

"He's a champ. He should get some rest now." She gave me a pointed look. "So should you."

Callaway nodded.

"Don't worry. I'll make sure she gets some sleep."

She smiled at him, clearly charmed.

"Thank you, Callaway. I'll tell Miss Bonnie you said hello."

He shook his head.

"I already popped my head in. She was too busy with her latest murder mystery for me. She's bloodthirsty, that one!"

Maggie had a good belly laugh over that one. I was watching all of this unfolding in front of me. Callaway was taking me home. Callaway was making sure I got sleep. Callaway was going to help take care of Tommy. Callaway wanted us all to move in together.

Callaway wanted babies.

He took my hand and squeezed it.

"We'll be back tomorrow, my man."

Tommy grinned and fist-bumped him.

"Cool."

"Are you sure you'll be alright?" I was practically begging Tommy to ask me to stay. But he didn't need me. He was okay.

"Go home! You're starting to smell."

He pulled a face and I laughed. I couldn't help it. He

might have just woken up from a coma, but he was still my pain in the ass little brother.

And I couldn't have loved him any more.

Love.

Callaway said he loved me.

He loves me.

I looked up at him as he tugged my hand, leading me out of Tommy's room. He was texting someone, but he looked at me and winked.

It hit me all at once. He really did love me. It was in his eyes.

Holy hell.

Mr. Big Bad Biker was in love with me.

I was too tired to think about it, but I kinda thought I loved him too.

The minute we were through the door, Callaway tossed me over his shoulder and carried me down the hall.

CHAPTER SIXTEEN

Callaway

"*P*ut me down!"

The delicious package slung over my shoulder was wiggling around. I shook my head and smiled. It wasn't a happy smile. It was grim and determined.

I held her tightly and waited out front for the cavalry to arrive. Every time she wiggled, I slapped her ass. I was too mad to speak and she was too tired to put up much of a fight.

Whiskey pulled up not five minutes later.

"You need a lift?"

"You mind riding my bike?"

"No, man. What's up?"

"Molly hasn't slept in three days. I can't have her falling off my ride."

"I heard about her brother. How's he doing?"

"Good. He's a tough kid."

"Hmmph!"

Molly was muttering something, so I swung her into my arms so she could meet Whiskey.

"Oh, yeah. Sorry, sweetheart. Molly, this is Whiskey. Whiskey, this is my old lady."

"Well, goddamn. It's nice to meet you, Molly."

Whiskey grinned. Molly glared at me. I pretended not to notice.

"I'm not old!"

I squeezed her. She was tired and cranky. We'd sort everything out once she got some rest.

"That's not what it means, sweetheart."

Whiskey opened the door, and I deposited Molly in the seat, fastening her seat belt. She pouted a little bit and my heart constricted at the shadows under her eyes. She must be wiped.

That was why she'd tried to break up with me, I decided.

I was still mad about it, but I was more concerned about her than anything. We'd speak on it at length. But not until she got some sleep and some food in her cute little belly.

But we were going to have *words*.

"What does it mean? *Old lady?*"

I stared at her, still leaning over her in the car.

"It means you're mine."

I slammed the door and used the keychain to lock it. Just in case she decided to be difficult. But she sat there docilely like a good girl.

"Thanks, man. See you at my place. Cool?"

Whiskey nodded and I shook his hand. I gave Molly one last 'stay put' look, got into the car, and drove it over to my apartment. She was quiet on the way over, and so was I. It was better that way.

The stuff I had to say was not going to put her in the mood to sleep. She needed rest. I didn't want her getting herself sick. And I needed her awake for the talk we were having.

Yeah, things were moving fast. But it was right. I felt it in my bones. Her brother waking up had changed things, sped things up. But that was okay. Hell, it was better than okay.

I wanted her under my roof now. I didn't want to wait until we'd dated for some length of time. I wanted her now. I wanted to ease her burden. And most of all, I wanted her in my bed.

Forever.

If Heaven was whatever you wanted, then I wanted a gigantic fluffy white bed with nothing but naked Molly in it. She could be wearing something sometimes, I decided. Lacy little see-through underthings that didn't actually cover anything. One of my old shirts if Heaven was chilly. Maybe a button-down with all the buttons missing. That way, it would slide open with the slightest breeze.

And if it was my heaven, there would be plenty of breeze.

One thing that I knew for sure—there were no panties in paradise.

I gave her a look as I pulled in front and put the car in park. She looked nervous. That was good. She should be. What she'd tried to do back there . . . well, there would be a reckoning.

Once she woke up, she was going to have to pay the piper.

CHAPTER SEVENTEEN

Molly

"*B*ed."

      I glared sleepily at Callaway. He was pointing at his bedroom, being bossier than a drill sergeant. I shuffled in there, feeling like I was walking through water.

"Lift your arms."

I grumbled but did as he asked. He stripped me perfunctorily, then slipped an incredibly soft old T-shirt over my head. Considering he was nearly a foot and a half taller than me, not to mention wider, it fit me like a nightgown.

It was so soft against my skin that I made a loud 'ahh' sound. I was too tired to even stay mad at him as he settled me in his bed and pulled up the covers.

He gave me a wicked grin.

"Sleep tight, Princess."

I blinked and closed my eyes. Just like that, I was out.

The smell of something delicious filled the air. I opened my eyes, realizing how hungry I was. My stomach grumbled as the days of barely eating caught up to me.

I had a split-second where I had no idea where I was. It was dark outside, and the only light was coming in around the edges of the closed door. I heard someone humming and making soft clanging noises.

Callaway. I relaxed instantly when I realized whose apartment I was in. He was cooking, from the smell of it.

The man was full of surprises.

I padded toward the kitchen and peeked inside, leaning against the doorframe. Callaway was cooking. His jeans fit him like a glove, showcasing his sexy ass and long legs. He wore an apron over his bare chest. I couldn't help but let my eyes wander over all that exposed skin and big, thick muscles.

Cool your hormones, Molly. He's just a guy, not a sex machine.

But he *was* a sex machine. He just happened to be a very nice sex machine who looked like the quintessential bad boy. The man knew what he was doing in the sack—and in the kitchen, from what I'd seen so far.

I scratched my hip, yawning sleepily. I wasn't awake yet, but I could already tell I was more rested than I'd been in weeks, if not months. Years, maybe. The truth was, I hardly ever slept all that deeply because of worry and stress. Because I didn't feel safe. Because I was alone.

It hit me like a ton of bricks.

I felt safe with Callaway.

The heavily-tattooed, motorcycle-riding, pierced to high heaven guy standing in front of me made me feel safe.

I shook my head, not ready to examine that all too closely. Instead, I tried to figure out what the hell he was making. The kitchen was controlled chaos, with bowls full of various things laid out, cooking utensils scattered over the clean countertop, and two pots simmering merrily on the 1950s-looking stove.

Now I really was confused. I saw the neat curved lines of taco shells lined on a tray, but the smell was distinctly Italian. Garlic, tomato, and basil filled my nostrils. It smelled incredible.

"Italian tacos?"

He turned, clearly not aware that I had been standing there ogling him. And his ass. Mostly his ass.

A lock of hair fell over his forehead and he shrugged sheepishly.

"I like mixing things up."

I smiled, suddenly feeling more confident.

"I can't wait to try it."

He stared at me, the heat in his gaze doing crazy things to my insides.

"I guess I'll get dressed."

He didn't say anything, just stared. I was starting to feel like a freak when he cleared his throat.

"You could take a shower. If you want."

I nodded and smiled, making a swirling motion with my finger.

"Don't let dinner burn."

He blinked and seemed to come back to himself. He shook his head and gave me an exasperated look.

"Yeah, I got it."

I was practically whistling as I grabbed my clothes and slipped into the bathroom. The water pressure was good, and I took the time to wash my hair with his yummy-smelling shampoo. I didn't linger though. I wanted to call Tommy, see how he was.

I tried to suppress the urge to imagine the worst-case

scenario. His going under again, being scared, alone as he felt consciousness slip away.

He's okay. It's over. He's okay, Molls.

And anyway, there's nothing I could do about it. Not even sitting there and staring at him every second of every day would keep him safe. That's not how the world worked.

That dark thought nearly sent me to my knees. I'd been carrying the weight of the world for so long . . . and for what? I was just a human. Imperfect and definitely not all-powerful. So what was I making myself crazy for?

I dried off and put my clothes back on, wishing I had something cleaner to put on. I felt a lot better, though, as I sank onto the couch and dialed the nursing home.

"Hi, I'm calling for Tommy Malone."

"Is this Molly?"

"Yes! Jackie?"

"Hey, girl. I'll call his room for you."

"Thank you so much."

"It's no big thing." A breath as she hesitated. "I'm so happy for you two."

I felt a big warm spot open up in my chest. We weren't alone. It wasn't just me and Tommy anymore. We'd made real connections since we came here.

As if on cue, Callaway walked in, bearing food.

He held up a bowl and a stack of plates.

"Food's ready when you are."

I smiled at him, the phone clutched to my ear. I nodded and mumbled, "Thanks." He started setting the small table by the windows where we'd used the laptop earlier.

I heard the phone ring a few times as I was connected and then a soft click.

"Yeah?"

I closed my eyes and pulled my knees into my chest. The sound of Tommy's voice was the best thing I had ever heard. By far. He was still here. He was okay.

"Hey."

"Hey, you."

"Listen. I'm sorry I'm not there. I'm coming over soon. I just need to eat something really quickly and—"

He cut me off.

"I'm good. Seriously, Molls, you need to chill."

I laughed, feeling every minute of the last five years. Every *second*.

"Chill. Right."

"Well, you do. I'm okay. I'm going to bed soon. And anyway, I could use some *alone time*."

I cracked up at that. My brother was a teenage boy and he was basically telling me he needed to wank.

"Gross."

"Whatever. Just get some sleep or whatever. Is Callaway there?"

"Yeah, I'm at his place."

"Good. I like that guy."

"You do, huh?"

"Yeah. And so do you."

I nodded, watching Callaway bring all the Italian taco fixings out to the table. He couldn't hear me, but Tommy sensed my agreement. I did like Callaway. Even though it scared me, I liked him a lot.

"See you tomorrow, Sis."

"Okay, Bro. I'll catch you mañana."

I heard the whoosh of air as he set the phone down. I set my phone on the heavy wood coffee table and pushed my damp hair behind my ears.

Callaway carried out a bottle of wine and two glasses. He stopped, checking in with me.

"All good?"

I nodded, smiling brightly at him.

"Yes. All good."

"Great. Let's eat."

My stomach made a loud rumble in response. Yes, we would eat. And after that, I wasn't quite sure what would happen.

Liar. You know exactly what's going to happen. It's about time too.

Tonight, I was finally going to lost my V-card.

CHAPTER EIGHTEEN

Callaway

"*H*ad enough?"

Molly was leaned back in her chair, holding her cute little belly. She'd been so tired and hungry, she'd put away almost three helpings. I hoped she hadn't overdone it. I didn't want her upchucking while I had my way with her.

Because I had plans for her.

Big plans.

I smiled reassuringly. No need to make her nervous about what was to come. She'd been through so much, it kind of made my head spin. She was so sweet and yet so strong. She broke my heart and healed it, all at the same fucking time.

All I wanted to do was keep her close, put my hands on her, see her fucking perfect face every day, and protect her.

Well, I wanted to touch her with a lot more than my hands. I wanted her against me as often as possible. It wasn't just about sex either. It was almost as if I wanted to absorb her, just lay my body on hers and get as close as possible. Not just with my cock.

I want to freaking mind meld with her.

Yeah, Molly was turning me into an alien from a Sci-Fi movie. Only this was the soft-core porn version of that Sci-Fi movie. If I was an alien, I wanted to mate with a human.

This human.

I smiled at her again, reaching out to pick up our plates. We'd both had a little wine, but not enough to make us act foolish. Just enough for a little courage.

The truth was, I needed it.

I was laying my cards on the table tonight. Laying down the law. I felt sure that my way was right, and the best thing for both of us. Best for her brother too.

But deep down, I was afraid she would say no. Push me away again. Tear me apart without even realizing what she was doing. I'd nearly lost my mind when she'd tried to turn me away. It was like the sun had gone out and it was never coming out again. I had been crumbling, and she had barely noticed, too tired to even pay attention while she ripped my heart out.

Because I knew without a doubt that Miss Molly had no clue how much power she had over me.

And she had a lot. I'd never let someone in like this. Never wanted to. But with her . . . she was it. She had more power over me than anyone, ever.

Tonight, I was going to show her how much.

I prayed to God she didn't run away from me.

"Thank you. I feel human again."

I shooed her away when she tried to help me clear the table. She was going to need her energy. Every bit of it.

"Why don't you go sit on the couch? I'll be there in a second."

I made short work of the mess, leaving some things to soak and sticking a few things in the dishwasher. I put the leftovers into Tupperware and into the fridge. It wasn't like I spent a lot of time cooking and cleaning, but I was no slob. Bonnie hadn't raised me to be disgusting.

Even my messy day after party nights got cleaned up within twenty-four hours. Not that I ever brought the party home. But I had definitely tied on one in my apartment or finished up early in the morning at home. Most nights, I crashed at the club house, usually with a bed full of club girls.

> *Man, those days feel a million miles away. And not in a bad way. I couldn't care less that my days of running wild are over.*

I dried my hands and leaned against the door to the living room, watching my quarry. Molly was reading a magazine, something I'd had lying around. She was so serious, so proper-looking sitting there. My mouth twisted in a wry smile.

> *She's a very proper young lady, and I'm about to do filthy things to her.*

Filthy, unspeakable things. Things she had never done before. Things she had never imagined.

As soon as we had our little talk.

"So."

Her head snapped up and she gave me a sweet smile. That smile melted my heart a little. But it wasn't going to make me go easy on her. I had to be firm. Otherwise, she'd keep pushing me away.

"Things are going to change. Starting now."

She blinked, her smile fading away.

"What do you mean?"

"I mean this morning. You said some stuff."

"You said some stuff too."

She crossed her arms over her curvy chest. I got momentarily distracted by her glorious rack before getting back to the matter at hand. I cleared my throat.

"You think it's you and Tommy against the world. That's over." She opened her mouth to speak but I held up a hand. "You have me now. And you can't just push me away every time you get cold feet. This is real. This is permanent."

She didn't say a word. Her eyes were very big and wide as she stared at me. Her gorgeous pink lips opened a fraction.

Damn, but I wanted to kiss that look right off her face.

She didn't believe me. Well, before the night was over, she would. I would make sure she knew it *real* good.

"I am buying a house for us. All three of us."

"But—"

"No 'buts'. I was thinking about doing it anyway. And now that you're in the picture, it makes more sense than ever."

"You can't just buy a house."

"Yes. I can. My business is doing well. I have a waitlist."

"But you can't spend all your money on me!"

"Yes, I can." I smiled at her coolly. "Besides, who said it was all *my* money?"

She stared at me. I stared back. I was still outwardly relaxed but my blood was pumping. I wanted her clothes off. I wanted her in my bed. I wanted to keep her in my damn pocket forever.

"You can't just tell me to move in."

"Yes. I can."

"What gives you the right to tell me what to do?"

She stood up, looking like a furious kitten. If she had hissed at me or swished her tail, I would not have been surprised. My lips curled into a smile. She really did look beautiful when she was angry.

"Because I love you. That's why. And you love me."

I took three steps until I was standing toe-to-toe with her.

"And if you don't love me yet, I will make you."

Some of her anger melted away. I saw it leave. Her shoulders relaxed. The fierce glare in her blue eyes softened.

"You can't make someone love you, Callaway."

I leaned in close, tipping her chin up so that our lips were inches away.

"Watch me."

My lips brushed hers and she sighed. It was a feminine, yielding sound. It said, 'I'm not going to fight you.' It said, 'I will let you take my clothes off and have your way with me.' It was the best sound I'd ever heard.

And I meant to hear it a hundred times before the night was over. Thankfully, it was still early, and she was well-rested and well-fed. So was I. And I'd been planning what to do the entire day while she slept.

Molly was in for a *big* surprise.

I scooped her up and hoisted her over my shoulder, my hand on her ass. It felt damn good under my palm. Juicy and so feminine. She let out a squeal, wiggling around a bit. But I wasn't having it. I spanked her, and she held still, probably more from surprise than anything.

"Behave yourself."

I squeezed her sweet ass and she let out another shocked noise. It was cute, but I wasn't going to be distracted. I lowered her carefully to the bed.

"Now, we're going to get a few things straight, you and I."

I wagged my finger when she tried to stand up. She sat back down again. Good girl.

"We are together. This is not a fling. This is permanent." Her eyes grew wide. "You belong to me."

She opened her mouth to argue and I hushed her.

"And I belong to you too."

Her mouth shut like a trap.

"So. Since you are mine, it's my job to teach you when you get off-track. This right here is what I call a correction."

I sat down and patted my lap.

"Lie over my legs."

"What? You're crazy."

"You're getting a spanking."

"For what? I'm not a child!"

"No, you aren't." I gave her an evil smile. "I would never spank a child."

She looked outraged, and I used her moment of distraction to pull her over my thighs. She wiggled but I just held her still until she wore herself out. I wasn't going to spank her hard. I just wanted to make a point.

Plus, I really liked the view from this angle.

"Relax. I'm not going to hurt you."

I admired the round cheeks as she finally stopped struggling. Then I lifted my hand and swatted her ass. I felt my cock start to harden as I watched her butt jiggle.

Holy mother of God, that was sexy.

"This is for trying to run out on me again."

Swat. Jiggle. Pause.

"This is for not accepting help when it's offered."

Swat. Jiggle. Deep breath. Pause.

"This is just so you don't forget who butters your bread."

She was laughing when I pulled her upright again. I frowned. Laughing? This was a serious matter.

"What?"

"Butters . . . my . . . bread?" She choked out each word around loud, unladylike guffaws. I scowled at her, then started to laugh myself.

"Young lady, do not make me spank you again."

That only made her laugh louder.

"That was the world's softest spanking."

"Well, I didn't want to hurt you. I was just proving a point."

"You know, Callaway, you're not very scary. Not like I thought at first."

I pulled her close and stared into her eyes.

"You thought I was scary?"

"No. I thought you were hot and dangerous-looking. There's a difference."

I started smiling and couldn't stop.

"You thought I was hot?"

"Oh, shut up, like you don't know that you're gorgeous!"

"Gorgeous? Hmm . . ."

I stroked my imaginary beard. But I was getting distracted. I needed to make my point. The spanking was only the first step.

"Lie down, woman. I need to do things to you."

My smiled faded as she lay down without protest. I looked her over, from the tips of her bare toes, up the long, luscious legs, past the curved hips, trim waist, and narrow ribs to her unbelievable tits, all the way to her sweet, perfect, prettier than possible face.

"Are you going to behave, or do I need to restrain you?"

Her eyes got really big.

"Restrain me?"

I felt my lips twitch but refused to smile. I held out a finger.

"If you aren't good, I will tie you up."

"Oh."

She was intrigued but not intimidated. That was fine. I wanted her gasping with pleasure and begging for my cock, not scared. I wanted her to admit she loved me, dammit.

And to tell me once and for all that she was going to stick around.

I started by running my hands over her. Over her clothes. I touched every bit of her, lingering the slightest bit over her most sensitive parts. She squirmed restlessly as I touched her, over and over again. I felt like an artist, painting a masterpiece. Using my gun to stain skin in colors and shapes that caught the eye and sparked the soul.

But I wasn't using ink or paint.

I was just trying to get her to soak those cute little panties.

Hell, I wanted her to soak the damn bed.

So far, it was working. I knew I was fucking amazing in bed, even without trying. And I'd made her come before. Twice. But tonight, she wasn't going to get satisfaction until *I* did.

I smiled grimly and traced the seams of her jeans. She was already horny. I'd seen to that. Ladies loved foreplay, and I was going slow as fuck tonight. She was going to *overdose* on foreplay. Each stage was going to last ten times longer than usual. And by dawn, she'd be begging me for release or riding my cock.

"I think we're ready to take these clothes off."

She nodded breathlessly as I ran my fingertips over her nipples, which were already poking holes in her shirt.

"Or should I start with these? Hmm, yeah let's just focus up here for a while."

Her eyes got wide as she realized I wasn't going to finish her off right away. But she didn't misbehave or argue with me. I toyed with her tits through her shirt for a good long while, ignoring the restlessly rocking hips just inches away. She was squirming, trying to hold back and failing. It took all my willpower not to pounce on her, but I did it. Finally, I pulled her shirt off but left the bra on.

And then I started again, circling, plucking, teasing until she was tossing her head and writhing on the bed. I wondered briefly if she could come from me playing with her luscious tits alone and decided to switch tactics.

I slid my hands down to her thighs and rubbed them lightly, up and down, coming close but never touching her pussy. She moaned helplessly in pleasure and my cock lurched in response. This was harder on me than it was on her. But even if it was torture, it was pleasurable torture.

There was nothing better than having her at my disposal. I could do anything to her at this moment and I knew it. It was the best damn feeling I'd had in my life. But I still held back.

My hands were itching to do more, press harder, touch skin. But this was the way to drive her wild. I knew it. I sensed it. Hopefully, I wouldn't completely lose my mind in the process.

I prayed fervently that the payoff was worth it. That she'd give in. That she would admit she was mine.

I lost the battle to keep this up and unfastened her jeans. I wanted to see those panties and I wasn't waiting another minute.

I swallowed as her sexy little mound came into view. The white cotton of her panties clung to her pussy lips, clearly outlining them. It was almost too much for me.

"You are moving in with me," I said as I tugged her jeans the rest of the way down. "You belong to me."

She whimpered but didn't say anything. I wasn't sure she was even listening to me. I ran my thumb over her cleft through her panties and was immediately rewarded by a damp spot. She looked so good lying there in her bra and panties. Her body was strong and supple and made for my loving. I decided I wanted to get her a white bikini and take her to the beach. Hawaii, maybe.

Either way, I was never going to forget this moment.

"If you want me to keep touching you here, you're going to have to agree with me."

"Mmm hmm . . ."

"Do you want me to stop?"

"No. Please."

"Are you going to move in with me?"

My hand lifted and her eyes popped open.

"I don't know. I can't think, Callaway!"

My fingertips made a lazy whirl on her inner thigh and she gasped.

"It's very simple, sweetheart. Do you belong to me?"

She stared at me.

"I've never belonged to anyone."

Her words cut through me like a knife. She'd been on her own for so long. But I couldn't stop now.

"Well, you do now. I won't hurt you. I'll keep you and your brother safe. I promise you, Molly."

"Okay." She sighed and closed her eyes again. I moved my fingers closer to her pussy.

"Okay, what?"

"Okay, I belong to you."

I grinned and leaned down to kiss her pussy through her panties. She rewarded me with a sexy whimper. I tugged them down with my teeth, growling at her like a wild dog. Then I got her bra off. There she was, laid out in all her glory. Jesus Christ, the woman was spectacular naked. She was the most beautiful thing I'd seen in my life.

And she's mine.

"Good. That's real good, baby. Can I hear it again?"

I kissed her stomach and looked up at her.

"I belong to you, Callaway."

"And you're moving in with me."

She sighed again.

"That scares me."

I lay beside her, letting my hands wander freely over her silky skin. I had my jeans on still. It was the only thing keeping me from plunging my desperate cock inside her. The big guy was desperate for her, to say the least.

"Why?"

She stared at the ceiling.

"What if you change your mind?"

Her voice was so tiny. So scared. She'd been alone for so long, and I knew this was something that had scared her since she lost her parents.

"Listen to me." I gently lifted her chin so I could look into her beautiful eyes. "There are only a few things certain in this life. One, that we all come into this life and we all leave it. And two, that I am going to love you until the day I die."

Her eyes filled with tears. I think mine may have too. But that didn't last long because we were too busy kissing. Kissing side by side soon turned to kissing with her long legs wrapped around me as I held her firmly in place. My cock wanted out of my jeans, but I wasn't going to rush this. I wanted to savor my moment of victory.

Before long, we were rolled over, with me over her, kissing and touching and, dear Lord, dry humping like a pair of teenagers afraid that their mom was about to come in.

But we were alone. And we weren't teenagers. And she loved me. I knew she did. She had to.

"Tell me." I nuzzled my face into her neck, kissing her softly as I breathed my question into her perfect little ear.

"I'm yours."

"Yes, you are. Tell me what else."

"I'll move in with you. Tommy too."

That was good, but not what I was after. Not what I craved. Then she changed everything.

"What else?"

I leaned up to look down at her. I'd never seen anything like it in my life. The trust and innocent lust in her eyes almost undid me.

"I want you to take my virginity." She blushed a bit and bit her lip, looking away. "Right now."

Holy hell. I'd expected that might be on the table, but I'd thought I was getting three little words first.

Turned out, those seven little words were just as good.

I squeezed her narrow waist.

"You're sure? Once I start . . ."

"I'm sure. I want you, Callaway. Please don't make me wait."

Well, hell. How could I say no to that? I grinned and kissed her lips hard. Then I travelled down her body, kissing and biting her as I went, soft little nips that made her squeal.

"Callaway!"

"Shh . . ."

My little Princess was going to have to wait for the grand finale. She was a virgin and I had a massive piece of equipment. I had to prepare her first.

And then it would be my turn to feel her wrapped around my cock.

I felt my cock grow even larger at the thought, if that was even possible.

I started slow, licking and tasting her puffy little pussy lips. She gasped and made sexy little whimpers as I went deeper, pushing my tongue inside her. *Fuck, she's tight!* I had no clue how I was getting my ten-inch cock into paradise, but I had to try. I used my tongue a bit and then switched to fingers, sliding one in to start.

"Oh, Christ. Sweetheart, you have to try and relax for me."

"I am relaxed."

Her breathy voice did sound calm. Shit. If she was so tight

I could barely get my finger inside her, we were going to be here a long ass time. I felt my cock leak precum as I ground my teeth.

Better make her come quick. Maybe get another finger in. Make her come and she'll open up.

I lowered my head again, licking and sucking her clit into my mouth. It wasn't long before she arched off the bed, shuddering her release. I doubled down, adding another finger. She had opened up, just a bit. I worked her, gently stretching her, my fingers getting all the fun.

My cock is jealous as hell, truth be told.

She came again, and I moaned in helpless pleasure, feeling like I was close to coming with her. It wouldn't surprise me at this point if my sweet girl made me come without even touching me. But I wanted to wait. I wanted the whole thing.

I slid a third finger inside her and pulled it out again, satisfied that I'd prepared her. I had a chance of getting inside her now. I'd go slow so as not to hurt her.

I wasn't sure it would work, but it was now or never. I'd been wanting this since the first moment I saw her. This was it.

It's time to make her mine.

CHAPTER NINETEEN

Molly

I was not nervous. I was ready. Prepared. Eager. Not even a little bit nervous. Not until I saw it.

I was thunderstruck when I saw it.

It was huge. Bigger than huge. It was monstrous.

Callaway has a horse cock.

Seriously, it looked like it belonged on a horse. Or a rhino. Or a freaking dinosaur.

It looks like it belongs in a damn missile silo.

What he had wasn't normal. It was a third appendage. Big, hard, and somehow impossible to look away from.

Callaway was on his back, kicking his jeans off. He shimmied them down and kicked them off. Then he rolled over and looked at me. He must have caught the fact that I was practically hyperventilating because his face got all worried and he rubbed his hand up and down my arm.

"Hey, baby girl. You sure about this?"

I knew he wanted me to say yes. *I* wanted to say yes. So I nodded, feeling less sure than I had before. He was huge. I was not. It was going to hurt.

But it would make him happy, so I whispered, "Yes."

"I'll go slow, sweetheart. Don't be afraid."

His gorgeous face was so serious, so solemn as he positioned himself above me. The smooth, flat expanse of his chest and belly pressed into me. It felt so good. Even the tip of his cock felt like heaven as it pressed into my folds. But then it inched inside and I felt like I was splitting in two.

"Oh. Um . . ."

I was nervous and he knew it. He stopped with his cock just inside me, holding perfectly still above me. It did feel good, but I knew it was just the tip.

"You are made to stretch, baby. Don't be scared. Just tell me if it hurts and I'll stop."

"You said you couldn't stop once we started."

He frowned, shaking his head earnestly.

"I'll always stop if it's hurting. I promise. It won't be easy but . . . Hmmph . . . I promise I will stop."

He looked at me intently, his jaw clenched as he held his whole body back. All that raw power in check. And he was doing it just for me.

"Am I hurting you, Mols? Please, God, just tell me. Because you feel like paradise to me."

"No. You're not hurting me."

He exhaled in relief and inched forward again. I gasped at the feeling of stretching. It still didn't hurt, not exactly. But I felt really, really full.

Maybe this is what having a baby feels like . . .

Why are you thinking about babies, Molly? Focus!

I let myself relax and slid my arms around Callaway's

neck. His handsome face was serious, his eyes dark as he focused on what he was doing. What *we* were doing.

We were really doing it. We were finally having sex. Like two normal people in a relationship. It was no big deal.

Except Callaway was an outlaw biker with piercings and a horse dick and I was an inexperienced girl with major baggage. He'd had dozens of women, I had no doubt. Maybe more. And now he was . . . what? My boyfriend?

Calling a man like Callaway your boyfriend didn't seem right. It was too tame. Too soft.

> *No, Callaway isn't my boyfriend.*
> *He's my man.*

The man braced above me was hard. Literally everywhere. Except maybe his lips.

He moaned as he slid in a little further. He was really taking his time. He did care about me. He wasn't going to hurt me.

"Oh, there it is."

"What?"

"I can feel your hymen."

My mouth opened. I hadn't expected him to say that. It sounded so . . . medical.

"I can do this without hurting. I hope . . ."

He angled his hips and wiggled around a bit. I nearly laughed, except that it felt incredibly good. So I moaned instead.

"What are . . . mmm . . . what are you doing?"

"Ah, fuck, Molly, you feel so good. Mmm . . . my buddy told me how to do this . . . without hurting you."

"Do what?"

"I'll tell you after. Okay?"

"Uh-huh."

He was breathing heavily as he worked, closing his eyes in concentration. Then something shifted inside me and he slid forward. If I thought I felt full before, this was full times ten. I felt an enormous pressure inside me, but it wasn't unpleasant.

"Oh!"

"You okay?"

I nodded. "I think so."

He kissed me softly. Then he lifted his head to stare down at me.

"I really want to move now, but I won't until you're ready."

I nodded and realized that it didn't hurt. Not even a little. I realized that I wanted him to move.

"Okay."

"Tell me when."

"Now."

He kissed me again, and I felt him pull out just a little bit, then push back in. Then he did it again. And again. Slow and steady.

And oh, my, did it feel good. Everything that had happened before was . . . well, it was nothing compared to this. His skin rubbed against my clit every time he went deep, and I felt myself getting close to coming again.

He lifted my leg on one side and wrapped it around his hip without stopping the sawing motion. He was so confident, so sure of what he was doing. And the look in his eyes took my breath away.

Pure need. Lust. Love.

For me.

"Jesus, I'm close." He stopped moving above me. "I can't believe how good you feel, baby."

"You feel good too."

He groaned and I felt him swell deep inside me.

"I can pull out. But I don't want to."

"What do you mean?"

"I mean I want everything. I want to have a baby with you."

"A baby?"

He nodded and pressed my lips with a quick kiss.

"Tell me, sweetheart. Tell me I can come inside you."

I don't know what made me say yes, but I did. Maybe it was the tingles spreading deep inside me, everywhere his cock touched me. Maybe it was the hopeful look on his face.

Maybe it was the way he told me he loved me over and over again as I felt him explode inside me.

I arched against him, shaking and shivering as I found my release. We came together, almost as if his body had told me what to do and when to do it. It felt so good. So right. I knew I had made the right decision.

"I love you, Molly."

I fell asleep in his arms.

CHAPTER TWENTY

Jack

"So, this is it."

Callaway stood there, looking like a weasel in a hen house. I shook my head. He'd always been the wildest of all of us, which was saying something.

And now the wild child was ready to settle down. In fact, he was dead-set on it. He'd even taken his girl's kid brother under his wing, helping the kid with physical therapy and wheeling him around town in his wheelchair.

They made quite a pair, a clean-cut kid who looked sixteen but was mentally twelve, and the tattoo-covered guy in leather and ripped denim who usually sported some sort of variation on a mohawk minus the shaved sides. Callaway had big hair. Almost as big as his personality.

But he and the Tommy had hit it off. And he was in love with the girl, that much was plain. Now that he was house hunting, I had to do my best to support him. Callaway might be crazy, but he was loyal to a fault and surprisingly good with the kids. He'd gotten the bug when he met Whiskey and Becky's girl the first time. And now the man had babies on the brain.

"It's perfect."

He turned in a circle, taking in the mid-century ranch house. It was dated and there was a lot of work to do, but it was a good lot on a quiet family-oriented street, with plenty of older SOS guys living in the area. A little more rural than suburban and not far from Donnie and Sally's place, right next door to his mom and sister. Spitting distance from the place I was secretly fixing up for Janet, in fact.

"How did you even know about it?"

"The house belonged to a club guy's aunt. It's a good neighborhood. My place is just down the block, and Donnie is less than half a mile from here."

"I noticed. Molly will love that."

"Janet will too. Those two have gotten thick these past few weeks."

And they had. Not that it surprised me. Janet was definitely not short on friends like Molly was, but Callaway's lady was a great girl. She was sweet and hardworking. The kids loved her too. We all pretty much thought she was a magician. She'd somehow tamed Callaway, almost by accident. She had succeeded where a thousand women had failed. And she did it without even trying, from what I could tell.

"Tell him I'll take it."

"You wanna haggle?"

Callaway had that crazy gleam in his eye he used to get right before a bender. He'd slide up to the bar and ask Donnie for an entire bottle. And now that Donnie's cousin Mac was manning the bar late nights, he was all too familiar with the look he had in his eyes right now.

It meant that Callaway was all-in. Not with partying these days. Just all-in with this house, settling down, everything.

"No. Just tell him I'll take it."

"You getting a mortgage? He'll need to see something on paper for that."

"Cash. I can give it to him tomorrow."

I raised a brow. This was whole-hog, even for Callaway. But try talking to a man in love. I just shook my head.

"You got it, man."

"Let's go work on those cabinets for your place. They still at Whiskey's?"

I nodded. "Moving them over to install in a few days."

"Perfect. I'll help you finish them up."

"You figure if you help me a lot with my house, I'll help with yours, eh?"

He grinned at me.

"Hell, no. You would have helped me anyway."

I grumbled 'cheeky bastard' under my breath, but other than that, I didn't say much. The cheeky bastard was right. We Riders stuck together. Even Crazy Callaway. He was my brother for life and he knew it.

An annoyingly wild little brother who had screwed his way through legions of women, but a brother all the same. He slapped my back and I glared at him.

"Come on, Jack. Let's get to work."

CHAPTER TWENTY-ONE

Janet

"We need to pass out these notices about shots and flu season."

Molly nodded, accepting the brightly-colored photocopies we'd made earlier. They pretty much said that if your kid was sick, to keep them home. Also, if you weren't getting shots, we reserved the right to keep the kids out of a class. That only happened when we had a kid with a weakened immune system who needed to be protected, but it had come up a few times and we needed to be upfront about our policy.

"I'll make sure everyone gets one when they come in and then check them off the list. That way, if anyone isn't in class, we can mail them a copy."

I beamed at Molly.

"Perfect. You're really good at this, you know?"

She smiled at me shyly and I was struck again by how innocent she was. How on earth had she ended up with Callaway? But she made him happy. And more far importantly, in my opinion, he made *her* happy.

"You're glowing." I blinked. "You aren't preggo, are you?"

She shook her head.

"I don't think so. But I really don't know."

"What do you mean, you don't know? Are you guys trying already?"

She turned pink and shook her head again.

"Not trying . . . but not being careful either."

"Wow. You guys just got together. It's only been, what, a month since things got serious?"

"A little longer. Callaway says we don't need birth control."

I crossed my arms and stared at her. I felt a responsibility toward her. Molly was already like a little sister to me. I knew Jack felt the same way about Callaway, so he'd be getting an earful from me later. He had to rein his 'little brother' in!

"Oh, he did, did he?"

"He says he's keeping me so there's no point in it."

"Keeping you."

She nodded earnestly. I knew none of the inner circle were pigs about women, but they could be high-handed with us girls sometimes. It irked me. Except when Jack did it, of course. When Jack laid down the law, it was always because he was worried or trying to protect me. Other than that, he pretty much let me do whatever I wanted.

Because Jack was just about perfect.

"All the Sons of Satan can be arrogant, but the inner circle is a whole other level."

"How do you mean?"

"Dev, of course, but he's President. Jack, Donnie, Whiskey, Lucky, and Callaway. Mac too, once he's initiated. They call themselves The Devil's Riders. And they are good men. But they are bossy as fuck."

She covered her mouth at my profanity.

"Let me tell you something, Molly."

She looked at me attentively. She was so stunningly beautiful it was kind of hard to believe. Her looks were pure and without artifice. She could have been plucked back in time to another century and she would look perfectly at home. And that look drove men absolutely batty with lust. It was just as bad as it had been with Kaylie. And when I went out with both of them together, forget it. It was like watching a parade. Or better yet, being on a float. All the heads swiveled to stare. And the few times we'd been out with Becky and Sallie too, it was even worse. It was almost like time stood still.

Jack said we were a dirty joke waiting to happen.

> *Three brunettes, a blonde, and a redhead walked into*
> *a bar . . .*

I sighed. Having beautiful friends was a trial, but I didn't mind. I didn't compare myself to anyone. My girls were beautiful inside *and* out. And besides, Jack was fond of telling me I was beautiful. Every day, and not just once. As long as he thought so, I didn't much care about anything else.

"My babies are the best thing that ever happened to me. I wasn't sure I was ready, but I *wanted* to be ready. Do you understand?"

"I'm not sure."

"I'm just saying don't let him push you too fast. You don't have to have a baby right away."

"Oh." She chewed her lip and shrugged. "Callaway wants one."

"That man wants more than one."

She giggled. "You think so?"

"Yes, I do."

"How do you know?"

"Because once I learned to trust him, he started helping out with the kids sometimes."

"Trust him?"

"In some ways, he's even rougher than most of the guys.

Wilder. And I've heard stories that would turn your hair white. But he's a pussycat with the people he loves."

"Stories?"

I shook my head.

"Not my place. But I will tell you without a doubt that he wants a houseful of kids."

"A houseful?"

I nodded.

"He's never happier than with children hanging off him. The man is a human jungle gym."

I smiled to myself.

"Of course, no one is a better jungle gym than my Jack, but don't tell Callaway or Whiskey I said that. They both pride themselves on being the fun uncle."

"Said what?"

I rolled my eyes as Callaway walked in and scooped Molly up into his arms. He kissed her long and slow and deep. I cleared my throat.

"Keep it PG, please. There are children present."

"Where?"

"Well, class starts soon, so there *will* be children present. Soon."

He grinned at me and kissed her again, grabbing her ass and squeezing it. Then he lifted her over his shoulder like a sack of potatoes.

"Any chance I could steal her a little early today?"

"I was supposed to help with the flyers!"

I shook my head and sighed but I was smiling.

"Okay, Callaway, you can take her. Remember what I said, Molly. Okay?"

She nodded and waved at me over Callaway's shoulder as he carried her out.

CHAPTER TWENTY-TWO

Callaway

"Okay, you can open your eyes."

I lifted my hands away and watched her reaction. She clearly didn't know what was happening. She gave me a tentative smile.

"Um."

I pulled her into my arms for a quick kiss. I couldn't keep my hands off her. I was already dreaming about getting her back to my place tonight.

"Welcome home, baby."

"Home?"

I held out the keys. She inhaled sharply and I smiled.

"She's ours."

She looked at the house, then back at me. I took her hand and led her down the path.

"I know it's a little rundown, but I just paid for it today. I'm going to fix it all up for you, sweetheart. For you and Tommy."

She didn't say a word as I unlocked the door and gestured for her to step inside. I flipped on a few lights and looked back at her. She looked stunned.

"What do you think?"

She wrapped her arms around herself. "I don't know. I mean, it's a nice place."

"Nice? This is home, baby! This is where we're going to live happily ever after."

She looked worried so I stepped closer and pulled her against my chest.

"What's wrong, sweetheart? You don't like it?"

"No, that's not it."

"Then what?"

She stepped away, looking annoyed. Actually, I was pretty sure it was the first time I'd ever seen that particular look on her face.

"You didn't even ask me."

My jaw must have hit the floor, I was so shocked.

"You're mad?"

"I don't know. I'm not jumping for joy."

"But . . . you promised to move in with me."

"Yes, but . . . don't you think I should have seen the house?"

I stood there, a terrible feeling in my gut.

"It's not that this isn't sweet or generous. It is. It's just . . . well, I want to be consulted on things. Like the baby thing."

My voice was deadly quiet.

"What about the baby thing?"

"I barely even had time to think about it. You just sprang it on me."

My jaw started ticking and I saw black. Not red. Black. She didn't like the house. She didn't want my baby.

"You don't want to move in with me?"

"I didn't say that."

"Then what?"

"You should have asked me! About everything! About *anything!"*

"You don't think I ask you anything?"

"Well, you don't! You tell! It's arrogant and it makes me feel like a passenger. It's not right!"

I closed my eyes. She was about to end it. I knew it. I couldn't face up to it right now. Maybe if I gave her some space, she'd love me again. Not that she'd ever told me in words.

"I'd better take you home. Let us both cool down."

She stared at me. "You don't want to talk about this?"

I shook my head slowly and she deflated a bit. She'd been riled up and now she just looked sad. Like she was disappointed in me. I'd let her down in my hurry to get us set up. It hurt my heart to see her look at me like that.

But nothing hurt as much as hearing she didn't want to have my baby.

"But we live together."

It was true. I'd gotten her out of that flea trap and into my place. There was even room for Tommy if he was ready to leave the skilled nursing facility before the house was ready. I'd thought everything was set. Planned. My timeline was in order.

- *Move In Together*
- *Buy House*
- *Take Care of Tommy*
- *Have Babies*
- *Live Happily Ever After with Mols*

Now all those plans felt like a house of cards in a stiff breeze.

"You stay there. I'll find someplace to crash."

"Callaway . . ."

She reached for me but I stepped away. I'd borrowed Whiskey's car to drive her over here. I could just drive her back, drop off his car, and walk to the clubhouse. There were rooms there for the guys to crash and do 'other things'.

Not that I wanted anything other than a stiff drink or twenty.

"Come on."

I knew the look in Molly's eyes would haunt me for the rest of the day. Maybe longer. She was hurt and I was the one who had done it.

But it didn't change a damn thing.

She doesn't want my baby.

CHAPTER TWENTY-THREE

Molly

"*H*ave you guys heard anything?"

I sat on Kaylie's sofa, staring at my friends. My new friends, who had done more than just merely embrace me. Sallie, Kaylie, Becky, and of course, Janet, were more than just friends. They had welcomed me like one of their own.

They were like sisters to me, and that meant a lot. I hadn't had much in the way of family. I had one now.

But I was afraid I was on the verge of losing them.

Even worse, I was certain I had already lost Callaway.

The thought of that big, intense, sexy as all get-out biker running around thinking he was a free man . . . well, it was enough to make my blood run cold. If he was with another girl, I didn't think I could bear it.

"You mean, is he under a pile of women right now?"

My lip quivered, but Janet wasn't being unkind. She was just plainspoken. She put her hand on mine and squeezed.

"He's not. Jack is keeping an eye on him."

"Whiskey too." Becky leaned forward, her pregnant belly

making her look like some sort of round doll. She was so pretty and sweet. "He said he's never seen anything like it."

"Like what?"

"Callaway is ignoring all women. Has been ever since he met you."

"Really?"

She nodded. "Yes, and I've been making him stay late to keep an eye out."

"You need him at home."

She raised an eyebrow. "You need him there more."

"Dev's been there a lot too. Probably a good thing, considering how soon he's going to be a daddy."

"What about Dev?"

A handsome dark blond biker was leaning against the doorframe to the living room. Kaylie jumped up with a squeal, launching herself into his arms.

"Hey, baby girl."

"Hi."

She sounded almost . . . shy. I sighed wistfully. Callaway made me feel like that. Each and every time I saw him, it was special. New.

And I'd gone and thrown it all away.

I was gutted, and at one of the best times in my life. I had my brother back. I had amazing new friends. And . . . I had him.

I forced myself to smile as Devlin waved and said, "Hi, ladies." before disappearing into the house. We all giggled. Even a tough guy like him was intimidated by this much girl power in one room.

My smiled faded pretty fast though.

"I'll be right back."

Kaylie hurried after Dev. She still managed to be graceful, but there was a bit of a sway to the way she moved. She called it her 'waddle' and even quacked sometimes when she said it. She was surprisingly funny for such a sweet girl.

She was back in a flash, sinking gratefully into the couch.

"He says Callaway is definitely not messing around. He's just drunk and belligerent but completely ignoring the club girls. They're all pissed about it, apparently."

"How drunk?"

Kaylie rolled her eyes. "Three sheets to the wind."

Janet nodded. "That's good."

"It is?"

"Yes, it means he's upset, not trying to get over you."

"Oh."

"So, you want to tell us what happened?"

I nodded, swallowing nervously. I was sure they would all think I was a jerk. I told them everything, from the conversation I'd had with Janet to the whole 'surprise house' thing. They all sympathized, with Janet blaming herself for the pep talk she'd given me right before the fight. I told her not to be silly. She'd been right, after all. Callaway was being heavy-handed, and I hadn't known how to deal with it.

I just needed time to come around to his way of thinking. To process all the new changes for myself. And I had. Now I needed to get him to believe it.

The girls had ideas of what to do. Show up at the club-house looking hot was at the top of the list. It had worked for Janet. Actually, that seemed like it had worked for all of them.

I shook my head. I needed to do more than that. I needed to prove to him without a doubt that I wanted to be with him for good. I leaned forward and told them I had a plan.

My plan was simple. And it would work. I hoped.

But it was extreme.

I took a deep breath and laid it all out for them.

CHAPTER TWENTY-FOUR

Devlin

"This is bad, D."

I shook my head, watching as Callaway slumped over the bar. Jack and Donnie's cousin, Mac, were on either side of him, standing guard. Lucky stood behind Callaway, casually making sure he didn't fall backward off his stool.

We'd had plenty of guys lying drunk on the floor, of course. Sometimes, they got stepped on. It was a bit of a ritual around here to take a piss on anyone who passed out too early. Not that anyone would dare to fuck with someone high-ranking like Callaway at the clubhouse, but they stood guard all the same. Donahue was worried about Cal. We all were.

My phone pinged and I saw that Kaylie had finally written back. I'd asked her earlier what she wanted from the store, and the list she'd sent back made me grin.

> Ice cream
> More ice cream
> Pickles

Salt and vinegar potato chips
More ice cream
Seriously, if you don't bring at least three pints of ice
  cream, there will be bloodshed.
Xoxox

"I'm going to head out. You think he's nearly ready?"

"Do you know their plan?"

"We just need to get him to his shop. He can't be totally wasted."

"He's definitely sobering up since earlier, but he's miserable."

"Yeah. Pretty sure I saw tears falling into his beer."

Donnie stifled a laugh. We'd all been through it with our women. It wasn't always easy getting them roped in, but it was worth it. We all expected Callaway and Molly to get back together.

Even Lucky tried to control his snark for once.

I was damn grateful the women had gotten involved. They were always the ones to come up with the best, most devious plans. I stepped outside to call my old lady. Her sweet voice always did something to my innards, somehow rearranging them so that I felt warm and settled inside.

"Did you get my ice cream?"

"That's how you greet your husband?"

"Well, did you?"

"Not yet but I will, babe. Promise. I'm actually calling because they're taking Callaway to his shop."

Her voice changed immediately. General Kaylie was in full effect. I grinned as she went from sweet girl to dictator. The woman was all-business when it came to executing one of her plans.

"Excellent. I'll mobilize the girls. Is he drunk? He can't be too drunk."

"Whiskey is feeding him coffee. And Donnie and Mac cut him off the hard stuff early. He has had about fifty beers in the past few days though."

I heard her sigh. She was worried about Cal too. Kaylie might be younger than the rest of us, but she acted like a den mother to all the guys. And Cal was special. Even though he was wild, he was fiercely loyal. His artistic streak made him a bit eccentric compared to the average biker, but in a good way. He was a special guy and we loved him. He was family and you worried about family.

Every damn one of us was worried.

The guy deserved some happiness. Callaway was crazy about the girl. And Molly loved him. She was a good influence, too.

I could tell by the way they acted together. They gravitated toward each other, just like Kaylie and I did. My wife was pretty much a heavenly body. That's how deep the pull was.

"Has he said anything?"

"No. Just that she didn't want him."

"She does. He just caught her off guard. He was steamrolling her."

My stomach clenched, remembering the time I'd caught Kaylie off guard and made decisions without asking her. I'd thought I'd lost her. It was the worst pain I'd felt in my life. I never wanted to feel that way again.

"Don't worry, babe. It's gonna work."

"I hope so."

"I'll see you soon. Keep that little bun toasty for me."

"Be safe."

"I will. You too. Love you."

"I love you too."

CHAPTER TWENTY-FIVE

Becky

"Okay. You ready?"

I glanced at the quiet girl in the passenger seat beside me. Her knuckles were white as she clutched the rolled-up piece of cardstock in her hands. She'd sketched it herself, with a little help from Jack and Mac, who both had a fine drawing hand.

They were the only ones who knew the details other than us girls. Jack had looked at Molly with a look of solemn respect when he'd seen what she was up to. It turned out the big man had a very soft heart.

We were lucky to have him. Whiskey told me he wanted him for our second baby's Godfather. Devlin was Petunia's Goddaddy, though Callaway was her honorary uncle. Sometimes, it seemed like all the guys were expecting to be a Goddaddy.

Truth be told, that made me wonder.

Did he expect me to have a baby for each of the inner circle so everybody could be a Godparent to one of our brood? That was a lot of babies, especially now that Lucky was back from active duty and Mac was joining the club. He was already family to Donnie and Sally, and now he was going to be official club family.

I groaned at the thought of all those babies and rubbed my belly. I was nowhere near ready to pop. Kaylie was way ahead of me on that. But the thought of having three more after, or even four if Whiskey wanted Mac to be a Godfather too, well, that was too much to contemplate.

Like all the guys, he loved kids, our kids in particular. Only Jack and Janet had multiples, though we were next. And we were hoping Sally and Donnie might have another, lord willing. They'd been trying long enough.

"Are you alright?"

I patted her hand.

"I'm fine, sweetheart. You're the one who needs support, not the other way around."

"I'm good." She nodded, as if convincing herself. "I can do this."

I exhaled and nodded. I was going in with her, just to make sure it was okay to leave her. I knew Whiskey was in there, and it wasn't like Callaway would ever hurt a woman, but I didn't want to let her go in there alone if he was upset and out of his mind drunk. Especially if he wasn't receptive to the little reunion we'd planned.

Callaway's tattoo parlor was only open part-time. At least a couple of days a week, he worked onsite at the clubhouse, where he had his own setup. This place could have made a killing if he trusted someone else to use his equipment. Maybe he would someday. *It's a very cool setup*, I thought to myself. He'd found an old barbershop that he'd barely changed other than the lettering on the glass window that read *Callaway Ink* in dark blue and gold lettering.

It looked amazing, truth be told. Retro and cool. Better suited to Brooklyn or West Hollywood than here. But Callaway had always been artistic. He wasn't just tracing patterns.

He only freehanded his designs, sometimes making them up as he went along. His talent with skin and ink was beyond anything I'd ever seen before. He was a good guy, deep down, even if he'd been a crazy playboy for a long time. I wanted things to work out for him and Molly.

I just hoped he was sober enough to hear what she had to say.

Or rather, what she had to show him.

We got out of the car and looked at each other. Molly nodded, even though I knew she was scared. We pushed open the door and went inside.

CHAPTER TWENTY-SIX

Callaway

"*M*ore."

"Uh?"

"Open your mouth . . . that's it. Drink!"

I groaned, trying to push away the hands. Whiskey's big ass hands were trying to force me to guzzle water. Eventually, he gave up and dumped it over my head.

"Hey!"

I was pissed, but he had succeeded in waking me up. I must have been taking a little cat nap. I blinked at him. It was early in the evening and I'd been at the clubhouse for days. Somehow, I'd ended up in my shop, where I had a comfy couch in the back.

When you partied as hard as I did, you needed a variety of places to crash. Crib. Shop. Club. Any would do. Especially when you didn't have someone to go home to.

Now Whiskey was here, forcing me to wake up. To come back to reality. And that was the last thing I wanted.

Because in reality, I'd lost her.

In reality, I was alone.

My insta-family had gone bust when I moved too fast. I

knew I only had myself to blame. I'd been overeager. I'd wanted to bring her close but all I'd done was push her away. But it still fucking hurt.

I knew I was going to miss Molly forever. I'd even gotten attached to her kid brother. I frowned. I couldn't abandon Tommy, even if his sister didn't want to be with me. The kid needed a man in his life. He trusted me. I didn't want to let him down.

Yet another thing that sucked about all of this.

But nothing touched the ache that was an empty hole inside me. A bottomless pit caused by the fact that she was gone. Gone from my bed and my life, even though she was still technically living at my place. I wanted her there, even if I had to sleep on this couch for all of eternity. It was somehow better than nothing.

She was in my bed. It was the next-best thing to being there with her. She could stay there as long as she wanted. Forever, even. As long as she didn't bring any guys over. That would kill me. But if she was there . . . it was something.

Somehow, I had a chance. A reason to see her again.

"Get up, jackass."

More water splashed my face. Well, it did the trick. I was fully fucking sober. Near enough, anyway.

"Ease up, Whiskey. What the fuck is your problem?"

He grinned at me.

"Solving your problems for you, ya donkey."

"What the fuck are you talking about, Whiskey?"

I stood, pushing my wet hair out of my face. My leather jacket was wet too. I sniffed it, realizing I smelled very distinctly of booze and cigarettes. That's when I saw her.

Molly was standing in the middle of my parlor, looking uncertain. Becky was there too. I noticed they were holding hands.

Maybe this was it. This was goodbye. Molly's beautiful

eyes were so serious that it cut through me like a knife. She was going to do it for real.

Whiskey had sobered me up just to watch me get my heart cut out of me.

"Hi."

I said nothing. I was too busy drinking in the sight of her. She looked like an angel, so out of place in my shop that it confused my brain. I blinked and realized she was nervous.

Molly was nervous. Why? Was she afraid I would make a scene when she broke up with me? That I would beg?

Well, maybe I fucking would beg.

I clenched my jaw. I would not make this easy for her. I would not lie down and take it. I'd fight for her.

She stepped forward and held out a rolled-up piece of paper. I took it slowly, not taking my eyes from her beautiful face.

"Open it."

I exhaled, finally looking down at the paper in my hand. It was . . . my eyes were not focusing. It looked like . . . a sketch. A beautiful line drawing of a heart with an arrow going through it. It could have been cheesy but it wasn't. It was almost folksy looking, like a tattoo from the early days. Something you'd see on a sailor who had traveled to the Far East. Something I would have designed myself.

There were three words in the center. They read . . .

Property Of Callaway

My head snapped up, afraid it was some sort of a joke.
"What's this?"

I looked up at her, suddenly unsure. What the actual fuck was going on? She smiled tremulously.

"It's a tattoo."

"A tattoo."

I stared at her, still not understanding. She nodded earnestly.

"Yes. I'd like to hire you."

"Hire me?

"Oh, for God's sake!"

Whiskey's voice boomed out but Becky immediately shushed him. I'd nearly forgotten that they were there. Hell, I'd nearly forgotten my own name, I was so happy to see her again. To be close to her.

Even if it was tearing me up inside.

"So. Can you do this for me?"

"You . . . want a tattoo."

"No." Her eyes were suspiciously watery. "I want *this* tattoo."

Understanding dawned. Relief crashed through me like a tidal wave. Relief and love and such a fierce sense of rightness that it nearly brought me to my knees.

"Oh, Mols." I crushed her against me, kissing her cheeks and ears and hair. I couldn't let go enough to kiss her lips at first. I heard Whiskey and Becky say goodnight and leave. I barely spared them a thought.

She was here.

She was mine.

We were kissing then, deep and wild and hot. But it was more than a sexual combustion. It was love. It was a deeper love than I ever could have imagined.

"So, is it going to hurt?"

I realized I was still holding the design in my hand. I shook my head, leaning my forehead against hers.

"No, sweetheart."

"Really?"

"It won't hurt because I'm not going to do it."

She looked confused and a little hurt.

"Why not?"

"When you are ready, I'll ink you. But it won't say that you're my property. I will never put that on your skin. I told you we belong to each other. It's not the same thing."

"Oh."

She turned pink and I let my hands slide down to her bottom.

"And I don't want to rush you again. But I *really* appreciate the thought."

I gave her a good squeeze and she sighed. She'd been missing me too.

"I want you so bad, Molly."

"I want you too."

"How do you feel about this couch?"

"What for?"

I gave her a look and she turned even pinker. Goddamn, the woman was adorable!

"Your bare ass, for one thing."

She giggled and nodded. "Okay." She gave me a saucy smirk. "It will give you time to sober up."

"What do I need to be sober for?"

"To drive me home," she whispered, "ya donkey."

I laughed and lifted her up, carrying her to the couch. I gently laid her down and started peeling my clothes off. She raised her eyebrows as I stripped.

"You know, you could take your clothes off now."

She shook her head.

"Too busy."

"Too busy doing what?"

"Enjoying the view."

I laughed and leaned over her, tugging her clothes away. My smile faded, replaced by a serious look. I felt so warm inside. So loved. It was hard to believe that I'd been so close to losing her.

And all I'd had to do was not push too hard. Give her a chance to breathe. She came back to me.

"I can't wait."

"Me either."

I climbed on top of her, kissing her hard and deep. We went from zero to sixty just like that. My fingers found her pussy. I moaned when I found her wet and ready for me.

"Mols, I want—"

She gripped my hips.

"I don't want to wait. Do it!"

With a moan, I positioned my cock against her slick lips and pushed forward. I nearly lost my mind at the feel of her tightness wrapping itself around me. Letting me in. Enveloping me.

She whimpered in kitten-like pleasure as I drove home. And then it was on. Long, deep strokes that brought us both to the brink quickly and kept us there. For a long time, the only sounds in the parlor were our heavy breathing and words of love.

But I couldn't wait. My need was too urgent. I thought I had lost her and now I had to have her, claim her, make her mine.

I tried to hold on. To be smooth and steady. I circled my hips as slowly as I could. But it wasn't long until I was thrashing wildly, our tongues tangling and our breathing rough. I felt a massive orgasm building up and I couldn't hold it back.

"Oh, God, Mols, I can't—"

"Ah, ah, ah, ahh!"

The unbelievable sound of Molly's orgasm tipped me over the edge. I felt her slick walls gripping my shaft, milking me of every drop as my lust poured out of me. I filled her up and kept going. I groaned, almost in pain, I was coming so hard.

"It's too much . . . fuck!"

I collapsed beside her, turning her to face me. The two of us barely fit on the couch. Thankfully, it was pretty damn deep.

My body was twitching for nearly ten minutes as we lay there entwined. I pressed soft kisses to her face and neck, my cock still embedded deep inside her. I wouldn't move. I couldn't.

Molly's eyes widened as I felt my cock unfurl to full attention once again.

"Already?"

"Yes, love."

"You're joking."

"It's been days since I had a chance to touch you. What do you expect?"

She slid her arms around me and adjusted her hips so I could slide even deeper inside her.

"I didn't expect anything. I only hoped."

I moaned at the feel of her and at the meaning behind her words.

"Mols . . . I wouldn't have made it without you."

"Shh, don't say that."

"But it's true."

She smiled and kissed me softly.

"You'll never have to again."

*M*y fingers strummed lightly over my favorite old guitar.

I tilted my head, thinking for a moment. Then I played the chord again. The sound echoed through the house. Softly, though. Our little angel was sleeping.

> *Little sister*
> *Won't you come out and play*
> *We always wanted you to have a little sister*
> *I hope one day*

I exhaled. It was too simplistic. But the song that had been dancin' around my heart was almost like a lullaby. A sweet, straightforward song. A prayer for a baby.

> *Little brother*
> *I hope you will come today*
> *We always wanted you to have a little brother*
> *Maybe someday . . .*

I'd fought so hard not to dwell on the baby that hadn't come. We had one. I knew I should be grateful for our perfect little family. I'd just always wanted more than one. I'd pictured two, or even three, when we first got married. Eventually, the disappointment had gotten to be too much. We'd stopped trying and thinking about it, but it was always there, hovering.

I'd had little signs lately. A few things that made me wonder. I'd taken a thousand pregnancy tests in the past few years, convinced myself over and over that a baby was coming. I tried not to let it consume me, but every time I was late or my breasts got sore, it did.

Lord knows, we were active enough. We didn't use protection. I'd even taken my temperature and timed things for peak ovulation. But so far, nothing. So we'd stopped trying. Not that we weren't busy between the sheets, but all the other stuff, well, it was too much.

We were blessed with our one child. Our perfect little Lilly. I knew it. We had a close family with Donnie's sister and mom next door, not to mention an amazing extended family. The club was everything to us. Lots of babies for our sweet girl to play with.

It was more than most had. I was grateful for it. But I couldn't help wanting just one more.

Maybe someday . . .

Actually, I had this crazy feeling that something was different. I thought about taking a test but I'd been sitting on it. I'd been getting that dangerously hopeful feeling again. Just a week late, and sore breasts. But I'd been wrong so many times before, convinced myself something was there that wasn't. For a long time, I had been buying pregnancy tests in bulk. But then I'd stopped. It was just too hard.

It had been over a year since I'd even bothered to take a test. I got a little superstitious around my period every month. Nothing like this though . . . nothing to make me *really* wonder. I sat up and set my guitar aside. There might be one or two pregnancy tests in the bathroom vanity.

I told myself I was being silly as I rummaged through the drawers of the vanity. It was pointless. It was just not in the cards for us. We'd been lucky to get one. And we might adopt anyway. An older kid. There were tons of great kids out there who needed homes. Jack had been a foster kid, and look how amazing he was. We'd talked about it and even bookmarked some agencies online, but always in some vague, far-off way.

Still, there was nothing quite like holding a baby.

And what if . . .

I felt the plastic wrap with my fingertips. *There!* It must have been all the way at the back of the drawer, nearly over the edge and into the back where nothing was ever heard from again. I pulled it out triumphantly.

An unopened pregnancy test.

Just one.

It seemed fitting somehow. I swore I'd never buy another test. Never wonder again. Never torture myself.

I'd just carry on. Put it aside. Give up hope. Or not give up hope, exactly. Donnie and I had talked about it. We would just change our dream to something we could achieve.

I stared at the test in my hand, feeling like this was a momentous occasion, no matter what the test ended up saying. I was still wavering, wondering if I should save it.

Just one more try . . .

I took a deep breath, sitting on the toilet and pulling my skirt up. I wasn't wearing panties, which made me smile a little. That was good. I needed the comic relief. I'd been hoping Donnie would come home early and surprise me.

Instead, there was a teeny tiny chance that I might surprise *him*.

I put the test on the countertop and washed my hands.

Then I got busy. I straightened the living room and walked deliberately into the kitchen, as far from the master bathroom as I could get.

I didn't hover, even though I wanted to. I wanted to stare at the little strip and will a baby into existence. I made myself wait five whole minutes, just to be sure. I even made myself a cup of dandelion root tea. It was good for your kidneys, and I loved the 'almost coffee but not quite' taste.

I walked slowly into the bathroom, then glanced at the mirror. There was a guarded hope in my eyes that worried me. I mustn't put too much stock on this one moment. Just because it was my last test. Even if it was negative, it wasn't the end of the world. It didn't mean we would never have another child. Adopting was a worthy endeavor, after all.

I inhaled and let my eyes slide to the countertop. I froze, not breathing for a moment. It was something I had only seen once before. After endless pink strips, there was something different.

It was a little blue plus sign.

Unless the test was wrong, or expired or something, the impossible had happened.

After all these years, it had really happened.

I was pregnant.

CHAPTER TWENTY-EIGHT
Donahue

I stared at my phone, feeling panic mounting inside me.

Come home now.
Please.

The texts from Sally were uncharacteristically vague. She also never really asked for help, not even when she'd been in danger. I knew her scumbag ex was not around. I had tabs on his every move, thanks to one of my cousin Mac's friends who was a private investigator. The guy even had his own hacker on staff.

It wasn't cheap but it was worth it.

My Sally was worth it.

Besides, after the working-over he got, he wasn't much of a threat. The guy didn't strut around anymore. He limped. And he wasn't nearly as pretty as he used to be. I hoped that made it harder for him to get close to women. In fact, the PI I hired had actually notified a few women about his past on my behalf. I didn't want that bastard hurting anyone else. Ever.

He was out of the picture for good. She was safe in this town for sure, with a couple of hundred unofficial bodyguards roaming the roads. And anyway, she said she was home.

So the cryptic message was . . . well, I had no idea what to make of it. If she wanted to fool around, she would have sent me a sexy picture. I loved it when she sent me sexy pictures. If she got news about her career, she would just tell me. Her singing and songwriting were taking off these days in unexpected ways, with collaborations across genres and state lines. She was even laying tracks for a big producer in LA, though she did her recording from her own studio in our house. She was a hard worker and so talented it blew my mind. If she wasn't already mine, a lesser man would have been intimidated.

But the truth was that I couldn't be prouder.

So then . . . could it be my mom or sister needing help? No, she would tell me so I could rally the forces. We had club guys from every walk of life. We even had a doctor. And the Untouchables had their own preacher. The guy was badass and rode like the devil himself, but his faith in God was strong and true. We were on good terms with the Untouchables and used him for lots of stuff, like weddings and funerals.

So yeah, I was worried when I hopped on my motorcycle and rode home at top speed. I nearly lost it on a hard turn. I was lucky I didn't skin my hip as it grazed the road before I righted myself. Didn't matter. My woman needed me.

She'd even said 'please.'

I half expected to see smoke or a downed tree when I parked and ran toward the house. I threw the door open and ran through the house until I found her.

There she was, calmly sipping a cup of herbal tea in the kitchen and reading a book.

I stared at her, blinking. My heart was racing as I tried to catch my breath. She was safe. She wasn't even . . . upset.

Or naked.

No. My wife looked . . . blissfully happy?

"Are you alright?"

She nodded.

"Yes, sweetheart, I'm fine. I'm sorry if I scared you."

"Well, what is it?"

"It's good news."

"Another tour date? Something about the record?"

She shook her head slowly, walking toward me one step at a time.

"Better."

"You want my rock-hard body to give you indescribable pleasure?"

"Better."

I opened and shut my mouth like a fish. My heart was finally starting to slow but I still had no damn idea what she was hinting at.

"What then?"

"Something we've wanted for a really long time."

I looked at her, my forehead scrunched up.

"Sex in a hot tub? Fuzzy handcuffs? Hot oil?"

She laughed.

"I said something *we* wanted. Not just something you wanted!"

I stood perfectly still as she slipped her arms around me. She took pity on me in that moment. I could tell by the sweet look in her eyes right before she told me.

"We're having another baby."

"You're sure?"

"Pretty darn sure."

I let out a whoop and scooped her up, turning her in a circle. She giggled and slapped my arm, shouting at me to put her down. I set her on her feet just in time to watch her cover her mouth and run for the sink. I cringed as she vomited, rubbing her back as she splashed cool water on her face. I grabbed her a clean dishtowel to blot the water away.

"Sorry, love. I guess that cinches it."

She giggled again. Her eyes got wide. And she power-hurled. Mostly on my shirt. But we were both smiling the whole time.

"That was the first bout of morning sickness. I guess that makes it official."

"Yes, you hot little mama. It is official."

We hugged, ignoring the puke, and then I carried her into the bathroom. I turned on the shower while she brushed her teeth. Then I started pulling her clothes off, kissing her skin as it was revealed. I knelt and pulled her panties off before kissing my way back up her body. She giggled as I kissed her belly and then her gorgeous breasts. She was so beautiful it made my head spin. I started to kiss her lips and she stopped me.

"Are you sure?" She cocked an eyebrow at me and I laughed.

"You brushed, didn't you?" I kissed her soft and deep. "Besides, it's not like you haven't puked on me before."

I pushed open the glass shower door and guided her inside. We took our time lathering each other up, kissing and touching each other. I took a washcloth and rubbed soap on it before gently washing her bottom. By the time we were clean, we were both breathless and eager to get to the bed. I wrapped her in a towel and carried her to the bedroom, leaving a trail of water droplets behind me.

I laid her gently on the bed and tugged the towel away. She giggled as I pounced on her, careful of her midsection, growling like a wildcat. Then I licked my way down her belly to her pussy and she stopped laughing. I took my time, even though I was already leaking precum. I wanted to get inside her, but I wanted to make her feel good first.

Hell, it was a point of pride to me. I wanted to prove I could still make my wife scream in pleasure. More than once, too.

"Try not to wake the lil angel with your sex noises," I said with a smirk as I lowered my head between her thighs. I had a good ole time making her squeal. She had her hand over her mouth when she came. I was grinning the whole time.

Then I slid into her welcoming heat and *I* was the one who had to stifle my moans. She felt so damn good. It was like coming home every damn time.

I tried to go slow. I really did. But my body took over, driving deep until I lost my rhythm and lost control. I bucked like a wild man, hissing love words between clenched teeth. And Sally was right there with me. She climaxed hard and this time, there was no silencing her. I didn't even try.

Both of us were loud at the end, and we were not surprised to hear Lilly's little feet pattering around as we lay there beside each other, covered in sweat. I laughed, still trying to catch my breath. Sally started to rise but I pushed her back and threw a blanket over her.

"Rest. I got this. She can have her dinner now, right?"

She nodded, snuggling deeper into the covers.

I walked into the nursery, looking for my daughter. I decided to move Lilly to a bigger room down the hallway a little way, and change the colors in here. Well, the soft lavender worked for another girl. But if we had a boy . . .

I grinned. My wife was against the whole pink and blue

thing. She was a fan of soft green and buttery yellows. And lavender, obviously. Whatever she wanted, I would make it happen. I cradled our daughter against my chest, pressing a kiss into her downy blonde hair.

We're gonna have another baby.

CHAPTER TWENTY-NINE

Callaway

"Tell me if it hurts. I'll stop."

"Shut up, Callaway."

I glared at the beauty in my chair. She gave me an exasperated look. But then she kissed me.

So I forgave her.

"Of course it's going to hurt. I'll tell you if it gets too bad. Okay?"

I'd already done mine, finding a spot just above my heart that had room for it. An intertwining design with our names and the eternity symbol, with intricate flourishes that elevated it way beyond a simple 'so-and-so and so-and-so forever' type of tat. You had to look closely to see what the meaning was.

But we knew.

And we'd both wear it forever.

It was funny, but I'd never liked giving this kind of tat. I'd turned down the work eighty percent of the time. The couple shit seemed like bad voodoo to me. I'd thought it was all just a disaster waiting to happen. I'd expected every single customer to come back and ask me to ink over it a few years, or even a few months later. But now I knew why they wanted it.

I finally understood.

If I could tat her name on every inch of my skin, I would. She was so deep inside me, it was on the cellular level. She was already in my heart, so why not my skin? I felt better with her name on my flesh. Secure. She'd always be with me now, every second of every day.

"Okay, sweetheart. Here goes."

I'd already iced her skin and dried it. Made her have a stiff drink. Everything I usually sneered at. But she was my woman, and I wanted this to hurt as little as possible. I'd do anything for my lady, dammit.

Even mark her. It was crazy but this felt inevitable. Like we'd been working our way up to this moment since the exact instant we met. It was sacred in a way. It felt ceremonial. It felt like a real commitment.

So I began.

To her credit, she didn't make a sound. Not when I did the outline. Not when I started to fill in the details. Not even when I started the shading.

"Want to take a break? I'm nearly done."

She shook her head. I knew she was in pain but she wanted me to finish. So I did.

Then I was cleaning her up, bandaging her carefully, and hauling her out of the chair to sit on my lap. Her tat wasn't in the same place as mine. Hers was on her shoulder, where it would be easier to cover up if she needed to. For professional reasons, of course.

The rest of the time, she'd wear it with pride. She'd even teased me about only wearing muscle shirts and tank tops to show off her ink. I teased her that if she showed that much skin all the time, I'd have to run around town cracking skulls because everyone would be ogling her.

Mols told me she loved the new tat. She called it her 'brand' but it was more than that.

It's a promise.

"You hungry?"

She nodded, curled up on my lap like a kitten.

"I thought we could swing by Mae's and bring something to the home."

I knew she meant for Tommy. We'd been back together for a couple of weeks and Tommy had been improving the whole time. The kid was amazing. Apparently, all the stuff Molly had done for him had worked. All that talking and singing and stimulation. She'd had the nurses play soft classical music when she wasn't there, though not at night, obviously. She'd held his hand each and every day he'd been in the coma. Just her presence had helped. Her voice had kept his brain working enough to repair the damage.

He would be moving in with us soon. I was working around the clock to get the house ready. So were all the guys, even Jack. He'd put his own dream house on hold to get us in our home even faster. And damn if I didn't love him even more for it.

I pressed a kiss to Molly's head and set her on her feet. I wanted her, but there was time for that later. She belonged to me now and slept in my bed every night. I didn't need to pounce on her when we had family to eat dinner with. But I would pounce on her after that.

Life was good. I had my woman and we were going to start a family together. We already were a family. The two of us would have been enough, but Tommy was the icing on the cake. A baby would be the cherry on top.

I was pretty sure I was the luckiest guy in the whole damn world.

CHAPTER THIRTY

Molly

"Would you like some coleslaw, Bonnie?"

I smiled fondly at Tommy. He was so polite. He'd made fast friends with Bonnie, even though she was in the residential wing and he had been in critical care all this time. They also had a hospice section but that was in a separate building. Thankfully, none of our loved ones were there. Now he was in a new room in the 'transitional' wing. It was where they put people before they got a permanent room.

People on the way in, and people on the way out.

Thankfully, Tommy was on his way out.

It was heartbreaking to see a kid in a facility like this. The residential wing was really nice, and Bonnie loved it, but Tommy belonged in school. Out playing. Having fun. And very soon, he would be.

He was coming home in a few short weeks. Hopefully, we'd be ready for him. I was working a lot of hours at the dance studio. Basically, anything open on the schedule, I wrote my name in. Callaway had said he would cover my balance at the nursing home, but I wanted to contribute as much as I could.

He was my brother, after all.

My heart swelled with pride as I looked around the room.

Family. I finally have my family.

That's what this felt like. Callaway and I on the faded green vinyl chairs, Bonnie beside Tommy's bed in her wheelchair. Not that she needed it all the time, but it was about a hundred-yard walk from her room, so Callaway insisted on wheeling her over in it. He was such a good man, I mused to myself. He took care of everyone around him. His heart was so big, it had room for all of us. I'd never have thought it the first time I saw him, but he was born for this.

Callaway is the ultimate family man.

"So, what happened in PT today?"

Callaway took a bite of his food and waited expectantly. Tommy was always making us laugh with his stories from physical therapy and around the home. He had a distinctly . . . teenage perspective on how things went around here.

"Oh, I did a new trick!"

"Yeah? What's that?"

"Well, they have these bars."

"Bars?"

"You put your weight on them to help your legs get stronger."

I nodded. "I see." Tommy had a twinkle in his eye, so I knew this was going to be good.

"I've been doing it for a while. Sometimes, I even take my hands off and stand without them."

"Wow, that's amazing! You'll be walking in no time!"

He grinned.

"Walking? Dude, I'm almost ready for the Olympics! Oh, so today, I figured out it was the perfect place to do dips." He pulled up his sleeve and flexed for us. "I'm getting so buff!"

I chortled, nearly snorting out the French fry I'd been snacking on. Callaway gave me a look and Bonnie broke into giggles. Tommy was being funny, of course, but the thing was, he *did* look better.

Tommy was no longer the waif-like kid he'd been all these years. I'd overheard a nurse calling him Snow White at one point. I didn't get mad, even if it did make me cry. He was so pale and still.

Now, he had pink in his cheeks and some meat on his bones. And while he wasn't buff, he wasn't scrawny anymore either. He was gaining strength and it showed.

"So buff," I agreed, throwing at French fry at him.

He caught the French fry in midair. Tommy winked as he popped it into his mouth.

"Mmm, grease! Just what this growing boy needs!"

I was laughing again, holding my belly and trying not to upchuck. I was full and happy. I was safe. I had a roof over my head and so did my brother. I even had a job I liked. I had friends.

And most of all, I had Callaway.

I laid my head on his shoulder and listened to the three of them talk, feeling like the luckiest girl in the world.

CHAPTER THIRTY-ONE

Callaway

"*C*atch!"

I tossed Mac and Lucky each a cold beer. Mac saluted me and popped the top, taking a long pull. It was hot and the guys were all sweaty. I owed them beer at the very least. Lots and lots of beer.

Not that I wouldn't have hauled ass for any one of them. Even Mac, that fucker. We'd nearly come to blows a couple of weeks before. Or I'd tried to beat the crap out of him but failed, mostly due to being shithoused.

He'd tried to keep me from drinking myself into oblivion during the almost-breakup with Mols. Not surprisingly, my drunk ass had taken offense. I reminded myself not to blame him. He'd been tending bar and just following orders. Dev had said to cut me off, so he did, like a good little soldier. Now he was here with the others in my time of need. And I really fucking needed every last one of them.

Today was moving day.

Mac, his cousin Donnie, Dev, Jack, and Whiskey were here. Even Lucky had showed, even though the guy had been riding me mercilessly about Molly. He kept asking me if she had a twin sister for him to bone. I knew he was doing it to irritate me and it worked. I did not find it even slightly amusing. I shook my head. Dev had told me I couldn't murder him. Dev was the club Prez and since he was also carrying my shit, just like the rest of us, I decided to do as he asked. Mac was the only real grunt here, still in the probationary stage of membership. But as Donnie's cousin and the new club bartender, he had a lot more pull than your average recruit. Hell, even as extended family, he was already in the family even before he set foot in the clubhouse.

Even my sweet granny, Bonnie, was protected by the SOS.

It wasn't so hard to imagine her in leather, truth be told.

I grabbed another box and carried it into the house. Our house. Nobody had noticed that it was all *my* shit. I grimaced. Molly really didn't have a pot to piss in. I wanted to change all that. Not only was the deed of the house in both our names, but I'd already started buying her clothes. I wanted her to have books, makeup, jewelry, and anything her heart desired. I'd forced her to pick out all the paint colors and light fixtures. She'd been shy at first, but once she got the hang of it, it was easy going.

I grinned to myself.

My woman has damn fine taste, if I do say so myself.

Jack walked past me carrying, I shit you not, a stack of five boxes. He looked at me with a raised eyebrow. I pointed to the kitchen. With a grunt, he ambled that way, looking not unlike a redwood that had uprooted itself from the earth and was helping me move.

The man really was a giant.

I laughed and set my box down in the master bedroom, then jogged out to get another. Just in time to see a car pull up. I saw a flash of red hair and knew immediately that Janet was driving. I squinted and saw that Kaylie was in the front seat. Molly was in the back, peering out the window at the house.

Hell, they were *all* craning their necks.

I smirked, wagging my finger at them.

"You ladies were not supposed to be here yet."

Molly smiled beatifically. "We were just taking a quick ride—"

Becky jumped in, finishing her sentence. "And we happened to pass this way so—"

Kaylie jumped in. "So we decided to say hi!"

I shook my head sternly.

"You were all being nosy. Just admit it."

They looked at each other guiltily. All of them looked contrite except Janet, who was giving me a knowing smile. I crossed my arms over my chest and looked at them.

"Everything was supposed to be perfect before Molly saw it. It's a surprise, remember?"

"It is perfect," she piped up. I smiled at her. She was so sweet and loyal. She was wedged between Becky and Sally or I would have pulled her out and put her over my knee for a soft spanking.

After kissing those luscious lips of hers.

I made a mental note to put a spanking on the menu for tonight. She hadn't minded last time, and it had made me even hornier than usual. That ass of hers was epic. Basically, it had turned me into a set of balls with an erect cock dragging a man around behind him.

"Alright, if you want to see it, you can come in. I was about to start unpacking so you didn't have to do it."

"But I want to!"

Janet got out of the car, slamming the door shut.

"Silly man. Don't you know women love unpacking?" She raised an eyebrow as she walked past. "Otherwise, how can we tell you men where things are when you can't find them?"

My jaw dropped and Kaylie and Molly started giggling.

Becky nodded wisely, patting my shoulder.

"It's not like you aren't going to ask her where something is fifty times a day."

"I am?"

"Yes. It's biology."

"Huh."

Becky nodded sagely and followed Janet toward the house. Sally and Kaylie were right behind her. I caught Molly in my arms when she tried to sneak past me.

"Oh, no, you don't!"

She squealed as I hoisted her up against me so that her cute little feet were dangling in the air.

"Callaway!"

"You're a bad little girl, you know that?"

Her cheeks turned bright pink as she played along.

"I am?"

"Oh, yes. And later tonight, you're going to get a spanking!"

Her eyes got wider and her cheeks got redder. She opened her mouth to protest but I stopped her with a kiss. A thorough, heart-thumping, toe-curling kiss that went right to my cock.

Yeah, I was once again a walking hard-on.

I set her down and took her hand, letting her lead me down the front path. It was the original brick, but we'd pulled it up and re-laid it in a herringbone pattern. Just like the picture Molly had picked out online. I wanted her to love every little thing about this house and I'd gone out of my way to make everything perfect for her.

Starting with the front door.

Molly's favorite colors were blue and green. She especially

loved mixing them together to make teal. So our front door was . . .

"It's beautiful! Perfect!"

She traced the outline of the honeybee doorknocker I'd bought her and smiled.

"You got it! How did you know?"

I grinned, shrugging. I'd asked the girls for help and they'd gone above and beyond. Janet had taken downtime at work to help her set up a Pinterest account, then put it on her phone. The girls had encouraged her to look far and wide 'just for fun' and she had gotten into the spirit of things.

"Just wait." I hesitated. "I wanted to get everything set up first . . ."

"Callaway, if you don't let me inside that house, I'm going to go crazy!"

I raised my eyebrows.

"*Sexy* crazy?"

"No! Nervous breakdown crazy!"

"Well, we can't have that, can we?"

I tried to kiss her again but she just laughed and shook her head at me. I loved making this woman laugh. I kissed her hard and fast before she could protest and then stepped aside. She looked at me, her eyes shining, and I nodded.

"Go on."

She squealed as I scooped her up and carried her through the door.

Everything got really quiet as we stepped over the threshold. Almost like the whole world knew this was an important moment. I swear to God, not even a single bird chirped. I set her down slowly and she did a slow circle.

"Oh, Callaway."

Her breathy sigh of pleasure sounded so close to the way she sounded right before she came. My balls felt heavy as cannonballs. I gulped, realizing me and my hard-on were going to have to wait. A long, long time.

Our house was full of people and the truck was only halfway unloaded. But the moment it was, I was going to have to shoo everyone away so we could 'christen' the house.

Every damn room of it.

Maybe some of them twice.

She turned in a circle then glanced at me. It hit me like a gut punch, the warmth spreading out from my belly. She loved it. I could tell from the look in her eyes.

"Do you like it?"

She squealed and threw herself at me. Her arms wrapped around me and I lifted her off her feet again. It was so easy to hold her up. She was so little and I was over six feet tall. I'd started calling her my little doll, which earned me an eyeroll.

She was though. She was my living, breathing doll. Perfect and sweet and all mine.

Whooping and hollering made us break the kiss. Our friends were laughing and applauding. Even Jack. I grinned as Lucky shouted, "Get a room!" with more than a hint of jealousy.

Molly's cheeks were red. I loved how shy she still was, even after all the filthy things I did to her on a daily basis. It was too cute. She squeezed my hand.

"Show me the rest."

CHAPTER THIRTY-TWO

Molly

*H*e'd done it. He'd really done it. This was beyond anything I'd ever expected. Anything I'd ever dreamed of.

And it was all for us to start our life together. But the details . . . the tiny little things I'd chosen . . . he'd done that for me.

Callaway had truly created my dream house.

Everywhere I looked, there were hints of things I'd picked out. Janet and the girls had tricked me into finding things I'd liked, spending hours with me picking things out for 'inspiration.' They must have shown him, the little sneaks.

I would never ever in a million years have asked for all of this. For any of it, really.

There are two window seats. Two!

There was one in the master bedroom, with built-in bookshelves and cabinets on either side. There a larger window seat in the front room, which would be cozily warmed by the radiator underneath in the cooler months.

Sally had made the cushions for both. All those years touring in sparkly custom-made costumes had made her good with a needle and thread.

I ran my hand over the cotton cushion that covered the bench in front of the bay window. It was the perfect spot to sit and make a phone call or read a book. You could watch people go by and see the roses grow up the low white picket fence that enclosed the front yard.

Callaway had planted roses. For me.

I sighed dreamily, hugging myself with my arms. We'd been unpacking for hours. The last of our friends had just left. Tommy would arrive tomorrow. There were still loads of boxes to unpack, but not that many. It wasn't like I had that much stuff. Callaway had kept lots of stuff from his grandmother's house in storage, so that was here, but he wasn't exactly a packrat. It was mostly kitchen stuff and blankets, along with some cool-looking mid-century stuff that he had, or planned to, refinish. Clean clothes were folded neatly in the drawers and hung in the closets, and pillows and fresh linens were on the beds. Other things had yet to find their place, but the basics were done.

This was it. I was finally home. For the first time since the accident that ripped my family apart, I had a home.

"Hey, you."

Callaway's arms slipped around me from behind.

"Hey, you," I answered, leaning back against him. His scent enveloped me. He smelled faintly of good clean sweat and leather. The man didn't ever have BO, as far as I could tell.

"Time to call it a day."

I nodded.

"You guys started early. You must be bone tired."

He made a noise of agreement and pulled me closer. I gasped as I felt his erection pressed into my bottom. His really big, really hard, burning-hot erection.

"Cal!"

"Well, you said 'bone'."

"That's all it takes?"

"*Breathing* is all it takes when I'm around you."

He turned me around to face him and took my face in his hands. He looked me over, running his thumb over my jaw.

"God, you're beautiful."

I smiled shyly, not sure what to say. He gave me so many compliments. I still wasn't used to it. His words caused a thrill to run through me. It settled in my gut and lower. Warmth spread through me at his words and his touch.

"Come on, baby girl. Let's christen the bedroom."

I squealed as he lifted me up into his arms, making a big show of tossing me over his shoulder. Then he pulled me to the front and kissed me. He loved manhandling me. I have to say, I didn't much mind it either.

He carried me down the hallway, never taking his eyes from my face.

I giggled as he nearly knocked into a wall and was forced to look where he was going. He gave me a searing look as he carried me into the bedroom. He set me on my feet and pressed me against the wall by the door. I gasped as his lips found the sensitive spot on my neck and his hands went right for my breasts, tweaking the nipples and stroking my chest through my shirt.

Oh, lordy, that was hot. I feel like a teenager getting felt up in the back of a car.

Not that I'd ever done such a thing. My high school years

had not been . . . normal. I was more than making up for lost time with Callaway though.

I whimpered as his fingers stroked my pussy through my jeans. Then he was tugging my jeans over my hips and taking my panties with them. He knelt, pulling the clothes off my feet and kissing my quivering thighs.

"Cal . . ."

"Shh, I need a snack. You wouldn't deny a starving man, would you?"

"No . . . ohh," I sighed.

My head fell back as he pressed his hot, wet mouth against my pussy lips, teasing and tasting me until I thought I would scream in pleasure. He slid a finger inside me and sucked my clit into his mouth, thrumming his tongue against it.

Dear Lord, the man was thorough!

I started to shake as the first wave of pleasure washed over me, crashing down and leaving me limp and satisfied. But then Cal was on his feet, his huge cock nudging itself between my thighs.

He slid into me with an animalistic grunt.

"Cal!"

"Hmm?"

"The wall?" I moaned as he started to move his hips in smooth circles. "You said christen the bed!"

He stared at me hard, his cock driving steadily in and out of me.

"I said the bedroom." His mouth curled into a half smile. "But don't worry. We'll get to the bed. The night is young."

My hands clawed into his shoulders as a second wave of unbelievable pleasure overtook me. I screamed softly as he drove into me faster and harder. My back slammed into the wall again and again but it didn't hurt. No, it felt perfect. It felt amazing.

"Oh!"

I came again, and Cal's big hands squeezed my cheeks. He had one in each palm. He spread my legs a little wider and bit my neck. I howled in pleasure.

And he kept going.

I felt him reach down between us and drag his finger over my clit. So he was holding me up with only one hand, plunging into me, and rubbing my clit.

"Oh, my God, Cal. What are you—"

I screamed again, this time really loudly.

"That's it, babe. Get it out of your system tonight. Because after tomorrow, you're going to have to be quiet."

I was almost blubbering with orgasmic exhaustion by the time I felt his cock twitch and swell inside me.

"Can I come inside you?"

His voice was gruff with need. I realized that I wanted him to come inside me. More than that, I *needed* him too. I had *let* him before, but for the first time, I actually *craved* the explosion of pleasure that happened when we came together. Something about his cock pulsing his seed inside me tipped me over the edge every single time.

And also, I wanted his baby. I wanted it so bad it nearly made me lose my mind.

"Yes."

He threw his head back and let loose, driving into me hard and fast. He stopped suddenly, holding perfectly still, then he went wild, thrusting out of tempo and grunting like a wild beast. I was just as bad, mewling like an alley cat in heat as wave after wave of pleasure crashed through me.

I must have passed out because I woke up on the bed. Cal was above me, staring at me with a look of concern.

"You okay, babe?"

"Yeah. I think so. What happened?"

"You blacked out."

"Is that normal?"

He frowned and opened his mouth, then shook his head.

"No comment. Can you sit up for me?"

I sat up and he handed me a glass of water.

"Drink this. Then get some rest."

"So we won't be christening the whole house tonight?"

"No. We're going to have to wait until Tommy goes to college."

I laughed and Cal raised an eyebrow.

"But if we get up early enough, we could get one more room . . . or two."

I nodded.

"It's a deal."

He lay back on the pillows and pulled me into his chest. I rested my head on his shoulder and sighed in contentment. Our first night in our new bed. In our new home.

I fell asleep with a smile on my face.

CHAPTER THIRTY-THREE

Callaway

"You got that, buddy?"

Tommy gave me a nod. He was using his cane tonight and helping Molly and me with the party. I told him to sit his ass down, but the kid was stubborn as hell.

Just like his beautiful sister.

We'd been here a week. All three of us. And we were doing just fine. Most nights, we ate in, but we'd gone to Jack and Janet's for dinner once. Next week, Donnie and Sally were having us over. And Kaylie had invited us, once the baby was born, of course. She was ready to pop though, so we were all telling her to take it easy.

She had that mama bear instinct already though. She always had. She might be young, but she mothered us all from time to time. Especially before any of us had women to look after us.

I smiled at Molly, who was sitting between Kaylie and Becky on the window seat. She was wearing a pretty floral dress, red with little white flowers. Her gorgeous legs were tucked up beneath her. She smiled at me and her smile literally lit up the room.

She was drinking a white wine tonight. Her second glass. I wondered how much she'd drank in her lifetime. This was probably the most she'd ever had in one sitting.

I hoped she got horny when she got tipsy.

More than that, I hoped she was in an agreeable mood. Because I had a very important question to ask her. I was pretty sure she was going to say yes, but there was no guarantee. But she was worth the risk.

Man up, Callaway. It's time.

I cleared my throat and looked around. Everyone was here. Tommy was in cahoots with me, and he had hidden a bucket of ice in his room with a bottle of champagne chilling in it.

Hopefully, we'd have a reason to pop it.

Hopefully, she'd say yes.

But what if she didn't?

"Everybody, I have to ask Molly something."

The room got quiet real fast. I looked at Mols. She knew something was up. I walked over and took her hand, bringing her to the center of the room.

"Molly, from the first time I saw you, I knew my life was gonna change. I knew I had to become a better man. A man who deserved you."

Her eyes were filled with tears as I lowered myself to one knee. I had a ring in my pocket and I held it out to her. It was a simple gold band with a solitaire diamond. Her eyes got as round as saucers. I loved surprising her. I just hoped it was a good surprise.

"I'd be the luckiest man alive if you'd agree to be my wife."

Her hand flew to her mouth. She hadn't been expecting this. Was that a moment of panic I saw in her eyes?

"Will you marry me?"

She took a deep breath. She swallowed. She lowered her hand from her mouth.

"Yes! Yes, I will marry you, Callaway!"

I shot to my feet, pulling her into my arms. I kissed her hard and lifted her off her feet while everyone cheered. Then I realized I still had the ring in my hand.

I set her down and took her left hand, carefully sliding the ring on. It fit perfectly thanks to Janet, who had tricked her into trying on a ring. She stared at her hand, then at me. Then we kissed again.

"Who is going to help me pop this?"

Tommy was grinning from ear to ear, holding up the bottle and a stack of plastic champagne flutes. Everyone rushed to help him at once. Mac popped the bottle and Janet grabbed the champagne flutes.

Mac popped it with one hand and started filling glasses while Janet handed them out. I held Molly close against my side as everyone came to hug and kiss us. Soon, we were all drinking and toasting. Well, except Kaylie, who had a glass of sparkling apple juice we'd bought for her and Tommy. Come to think of it, looked like Sally was drinking the soft stuff too.

We all sat down again, the room full of happy people talking all at the same time. A couple of kids ran around the room, with Janet's twins sitting at Molly's feet, staring at her ring.

Suddenly, everything changed.

"Dev?"

Kaylie's sweet voice rang out and he was at her side in an instant. She sounded worried. We all turned to look at her.

"I think I just ruined your chair, guys. My water broke."

Molly ran to her side.

"Don't be silly. It's just a chair. You're having a baby!"

Kaylie looked pale.

"Yes, I am. Right now, it looks like."

Devlin slipped her jacket over her shoulders and hoisted her purse onto his arm.

"Come on, love. Let's go."

CHAPTER THIRTY-FOUR

Molly

*F*our men in leather were pacing back and fourth. Devlin was in the delivery room with Kaylie, and Jack had taken up a spot on the wall. He was the only one not pacing. Well, except Lucky, who was snoring loudly, slumped over in a corner seat. Apparently, he'd still been hung over when he got the call, which is why he'd been late for our party. But he was a Devil's Rider, so he was here.

Becky and I exchanged an eye roll.

You would think the rest of them were the ones who were about to give birth!

It warmed my heart though. They all went for each others' deliveries. If Cal and I had a baby, they would all be there, waiting. Kaylie was the Prez's old lady, and this was his first child, so this was an extra-special occasion. He'd been the first to partner off, and Kaylie had been like a little sister (and a den mother) to all of them. She was the First Lady of the club, and she was about to have her first baby.

Not that any of that mattered to me. I was just happy for my friend. Childbirth was a complicated thing, and there was always a bit of worry involved, but I refused to give into it.

Lord only knew what was happening in there. We were all trying not to worry.

Well, the girls were anyway. The guys all appeared to be extremely worried, Jack and Lucky notwithstanding.

My phone pinged.

> *You would think Kaylie was giving birth to a*
> *custom Hog.*

I giggled. Janet was so funny. It was a group text and Sally was the next to respond.

> *Or a very large bottle of tequila.*

Becky snorted a laugh and we all hid our smiles. I watched the guys circle each other. Mac and Callaway accidentally bumped shoulders in passing and nearly growled at each other. Honestly, they were acting like a pack of wolves!

"Enough!"

Janet stood and glared at each of them. As Jack's wife, she was the second-highest ranking of all the girls. Not that she ever pulled rank, but she did have a bossy side. She pointed at Donnie.

"You. Go get snacks and water for everyone."

She pointed at Mac.

"You go with him. Callaway, sit your ass down. Whiskey, go check on the bikes and take Becky for some air." Last, she pointed at her husband. "You, carry on holding the building up."

Then she waited until everyone sprang into action and very slowly sat down. The girls broke into applause as Whiskey took Becky's hand and tucked it into his arm. Then they left too.

Jack was smiling the whole damn time.

"All hail the Queen," I joked, and Janet winked at me.

Fewer than twenty minutes later, everyone was back, no one was pacing, and we were all eating junk food and chips from the dining hall. Everyone except Janet and Sally. Janet because she was extremely health-conscious and Sally because, as she'd whispered to me softly a few minutes ago, she was finally expecting and wouldn't put anything that wasn't organic near her lips.

I'd squeezed her hand in silent celebration.

The room got quiet. Jack stood up from where he was leaning against the wall, and I swore I heard the building groan from the sudden loss of a support beam. I looked around to see everyone staring at the double doors that led to the delivery wing.

Dev stood there, holding a box of cigars.

"It's a boy!"

Everyone went nuts. Even Lucky woke up and congratulated Devlin. The guys all accepted a cigar, though Janet reminded them they'd have to wait to go outside to smoke them. Then we all hurried down the hallway to see Kaylie. She looked stunning, fresh-faced and joyful, holding a tiny bundle in her arms. Her hair was a little messier than usual but that was it.

The woman was unfairly perfect, and if I didn't love her so much, I might have been jealous of how angelic she looked!

She smiled when she saw us, and we crowded around, wanting a look. She tugged the blanket down a bit so we could see his face. He was perfect. Tiny and red, but perfect. I could already tell he was going to be a heartbreaker.

"We named him John."

Devlin smiled at her, putting his arm around her and beaming.

"After my brother."

"He's perfect," I murmured to Kaylie when it was my turn to lean over.

She smiled happily.

"I know."

Later, when we were at home alone and curled up in bed, Callaway told me how badly he'd always wanted a family of his own. Like me, he'd grown up without parents. It wasn't that he didn't love Bonnie. He did, and he knew he was lucky to have her. But he wanted what everyone else had.

Every television show, every movie, everywhere you looked, there were two parents and a kid or two. He whispered to me that he wanted more than two. I laughed and told him to slow his roll.

He attacked me, rolling me to my back. He caught my hands in his, holding them above my head.

"Slow my roll?"

"Yes."

I wiggled, trying to get away from his hot lips where they pressed against my neck. He just laughed, giving me tiny little kisses that tickled. He breathed into my ear, and I squealed, my whole body breaking out in goosebumps.

That's when I felt it.

Callaway was hard again.

"Cal!"

"What?"

"But we just . . ."

He grinned at me.

"Like I said, I want it all." He leaned down to kiss me. "And I want it *all the time*."

He released my hands, and I slid them around his neck as he started making love to me.

"You're lucky then."

He didn't lift his head as he worked his way down my body, kissing as he went. Finally, he looked up, playing idly with my nipple.

"Why's that?"

"Because I want it all too."

He grinned and gave me a little love bite.

"I love you, soon-to-be Mrs. Molly Callaway."

"I love you too."

SIX MONTHS LATER

Callaway

"*T*here's no reason to wait. We should do it now. Today."

I waved the marriage license in the air. Molly was in college and so busy with school and Tommy, even though I helped a lot with her kid brother. And for the past few days, I'd had a strong feeling she wasn't telling me something. I had a feeling I knew what it was.

Her cute little pajamas had given her away. She usually wore these little camisoles and short sets to sleep. They drove me absolutely crazy. They were so close to naked, but far too covered up.

And usually, the tops hung loosely over the waistband of the shorts.

But not lately.

Lately, they were riding up. Her normally flat tummy had started to stick out. Just a little bit.

To tell the truth, it was sexy as hell. So were her swelling breasts. I was almost a hundred percent sure she was pregnant . . . or hitting the donut shop near her college really, really hard.

Either way, I liked it a lot.

I had been sitting on the feeling for almost a week now, waiting for her to tell me. I wanted to get married first. I'd been waiting six months for her to think it was the "right time" and this was it.

Our baby was not being born out of wedlock, dammit! Not that I cared about that shit. Not for anyone else. But for my little girl or boy?

Fuck no. Things were not going down like that.

"Are you serious?"

Molly had her hair in a bun with a pencil sticking through it. She was wearing floral sweatpants and a tank top that clung to her curves.

Her juicier-than-ever, brand-spanking-new curves.

She must think I was an idiot.

"Yes, I'm serious. It's time."

"But we can't just get married. We have to plan it."

"Yes, we can. I already called Preacher from the Untouchables. He's happy to do a fly-by wedding. Gives him a chance to ride fast and look at pretty girls, the bastard."

She giggled, then she sobered. "You really *are* serious."

"Yes. I am."

"Why now? I thought we were going to plan everything."

I sat beside her in the window seat and pulled her into my lap.

"It's okay if you're scared. We're going to do this together."

I put my hand on her belly so she knew what I was talking about.

"Do what? The wedding?"

I stared at her. She wasn't being cute. She just . . .

Holy hell. She doesn't know.

I cleared my throat. I didn't want to freak her out. I'd better ease into it, let her come to the right conclusion.

"How are you feeling lately, sweetheart? Any different?"

"I have been pretty tired lately, I guess. And hungrier than usual."

"And what about these gorgeous melons?"

She giggled as I fondled her breasts. Then she swatted me away when I gave her a gentle squeeze.

"Ow!"

"Sore?"

"Ugh, yes!"

"What about nausea? Have you been feeling sick?"

She looked at me and blinked.

"Did you hear me?"

"Hear what?"

"Hear me puking? I tried to be quiet. I guess I ate something bad and—"

"Shh. Sweetheart, I don't think it was something you ate."

She stared at me.

"Then what?"

I stared right back, my eyes telling her that it was something else entirely. I rubbed her tummy again. She looked down and then back up at me.

Then she jumped clean off my lap.

"Oh, my GOD!"

I smiled at her and patted my lap.

"It's okay, sweetheart. Come sit."

"I am such an idiot!"

"No, you're not. It's not like you've ever been pregnant before."

"I should be taking . . . vitamins! And stuff!"

"It's okay. We'll get all that. Let's just take a test first."

"Okay, I'll go to the drug store."

I smiled sheepishly.

"I already have some. In the hall closet."

She stared at me and shook her head slowly.

"You knew before I did."

"Looks that way. So, you want to take the test?"

She nodded and I followed her down the hall. I stood outside the door while she used the test. She was way too shy to pee with the door open. I kind of wanted to see her pee, but I didn't tell her that.

She would have just called me a pervert. And the truth was, she would be right. I *was* a filthy, dirty pervert, but only where she was involved.

It's been like that from the first moment I laid eyes on her.

The door opened and Molly stood there. She looked over her shoulder at the stick sitting on the countertop. Very slowly, we walked over to it together. We stared, not looking away as the little minus sign slowly turned into a plus.

I held her tightly, kissing her lips over and over again. Finally, I let go and she rested her head against my chest. I was gonna be a daddy.

"So, how about that last-minute wedding?"

That's how I ended up standing on Jack's roof deck a couple of days later, wearing a black suit. I was surrounded by the inner circle and a few other club guys. Preacher was there, drinking way too much tequila for a man of the cloth, even if the cloth was leather in his case. Tommy was the ringbearer, and we had loads of flower girls. He could walk now and was attending high school, though he was a couple of years behind. He had tutors and was taking extra classes and attending summer school to catch up.

He'd end up graduating a year or two behind where he would have. It was good enough. He was going to be okay.

He was wearing a gray suit jacket and jeans. He had a little flower in his jacket, just like the rest of the guys. We were ready. The girls, however, were nowhere to be found.

Molly hadn't agreed to marry me that day. But she had agreed to marry me three days later. Jack and Janet had gone all out. The loft was tricked out below with tables and chairs surrounding an impromptu dance floor. The roof deck always looked festive with the string lights, but they'd gone above and beyond. Twinkling lights, flowers, and white bunting were everywhere.

Honestly, I can't really believe they pulled it off so fast. But I owed them everything for doing it. I would give them anything, including a kidney.

Anything but my bride.

A redheaded little boy ran up and whispered in Preacher's ear. He nodded and we all got into position. Mac played his guitar softly as we all turned to look at the stairs that opened onto the roof deck.

A soft breeze made the lights swing just so. It was the perfect night. We were lucky, I thought, just as the door swung open.

And then I ceased to think at all.

An angel was floating toward me. Her long, dark hair was loose, with flowers woven through it. Her beautiful face was serene, with just a hint of makeup. Her lips were extra-rosy and there was just a touch of shadow and liner around her gorgeous blue eyes. The dress was white silk, and it clung to her curves. She held a bouquet dripping with white flowers in her perfect little hands.

My mouth went dry as she walked toward me. My mouth must have been open because when she took her place beside me, she gently reached out and lifted my chin to close it. I smiled at her, feeling like a dope. The luckiest damn idiot in the entire world.

Then the ceremony began.

"We are gathered here today to bind these two in marriage. This filthy degenerate with this exquisite young beauty. Now, Miss, I have to tell you that you do not have to go through with this. There are always other fish in the sea, and if you like an older man in leather, there are plenty of options."

I growled at the cheeky bastard and he winked at me. Molly giggled.

"Get on with it, Preacher."

He looked at Molly.

"Are you sure, sweetheart?"

"I'm sure."

He sighed dramatically.

"You always were a lucky bastard, Callaway."

I smiled at him, feeling magnanimous. Molly hadn't hesitated. She loved *me*. Preacher had a way with the ladies. He was in his late forties and wore his hair long, and his beard was pure white. Apparently, he turned down as many women as I did, and that was saying something.

"I know it, Santa Claus."

He laughed at me, but I knew he'd make me pay for it later.

"Do you, young Callaway, take this flawless creature to be your wife?"

"I do."

"And do you, you beautiful angel, take this disreputable man to be your husband?"

"Yes, I do."

Molly was trying not to giggle.

He sighed mournfully.

"Then, I have no choice. I must pronounce you man and wife."

The crowd whooped and hollered as I kissed her. I was shocked when Preacher pulled her against him and kissed her soundly. He set a surprised Molly on her feet and winked at me as he headed to the bar.

"That's for not waiting for permission."

I glared at his back, ready to do murder.

A heavy hand landed on my shoulder.

"Shake it off, 'young Callaway'."

I looked at Jack then back at Preacher.

"Do you think he'd survive if I threw him off the roof?"

"Can't let you do that. Too many custom motorcycles parked downstairs. You might hurt one."

I laughed and we shook hands. I was quickly surrounded by well-wishers. Children were weaving around between our legs, playing a game of tag. Champagne and drinks were handed out. Photos were taken. And then it was time to go downstairs and eat.

The string lights were hanging down here too. Jack and Janet had mostly moved into the new house and were deciding what to do with this place. It made one hell of an event venue, and I told them that.

The high ceilings and old windows, molding, and gorgeous wood floors . . . it felt like we were in a loft in New York City. Something you'd see on TV with rich folks hanging around, eating strange food and talking about their stock portfolios and summer houses. It was more than we could have asked for, especially with three days' notice.

In fact, it was pretty much a miracle.

Everyone ate, and then Mac and Donnie did some light DJing. Then it was time for the toasts and I prepared for some brutal teasing. Molly looked adorably shocked as the stories started coming out. I cringed a time or two but it wasn't too bad. Anyway, my colorful past was firmly behind me.

First, Whiskey roasted me. Then Donnie roasted me. Even quiet Mac roasted me, though it was brief. Thankfully, Jack refused to let Lucky anywhere near the mic. That would have been a disaster. But then Jack and Dev made up for it.

"Callaway is a good man, and he's going to be a good husband and father. I love him like a brother. Congratulations, little brother."

I laughed and cheered as the giant took his seat. It was the shortest wedding toast in the world, but in my opinion, it was also the best. Then it was Dev's turn.

"Molly is already like family to us. Tommy too." I turned to see Molly's brother turn red. He idolized Devlin, just like the rest of us did. "We are unusually blessed in the people we spend every day with. Callaway is one of a kind. There were times I worried that he wouldn't grow up. All it took was one look at you, Molly, and he changed. He became the man we all knew he could be. There was an empty spot inside him and you filled it. We're glad to call you both family."

I looked at Molly. She was sitting beside me, holding a champagne glass. Hers had sparkling water in it, though nobody could tell. We weren't ready to tell folks about the baby yet. But soon.

She was so beautiful it took my breath away.

The room erupted in cheers and we waved. I pulled her chair even closer to mine and wrapped my arm around her slender waist.

"Sweetheart?"

"Yes?"

"Why don't we sneak out of here? We could leave early for the honeymoon. Stop at home and have a little alone time . . ."

"Honeymoon?"

I smiled. I'd kept that part a secret too.

"I thought we'd just go someplace casual. No big deal.

"Casual?"

"Uh-huh. How does Hawaii sound?"

"Hawaii?"

"Yes. For a week or two."

Her eyes got wide.

"But Tommy! And . . . school!"

"It's all taken care of. He's going to crash at Donnie's for a few weeks. And I talked to all your professors. They can email you the assignments. How do you feel about studying on the beach?"

She nodded eagerly.

"Yes, please! I've never been anywhere nice. This is . . . thank you so much."

She kissed me so sweetly I felt like I might float off my seat. I'd never been this happy in my life. I'd never felt so blessed.

"Kiss me again, sweetheart. And tell me you love me."

She tilted her head and our lips met. She was so sweet and gentle. She looked so perfect.

Something about her always made me want to mess up her hair. Not with my hands but from her head rubbing on the pillows while I had my way with her.

"I love you, Callaway. I love you more than I ever thought possible."

"I love you, sweetheart. I'll love you until the day I die, and afterward too. I'm yours for all eternity."

She giggled, her arms still around my neck.

"Okay, then."

"Okay, what?"

"Okay, let's get out of here."

We waited until the cake was served. We made a big show

of cutting it. Then she made a big show of getting some on my shirt.

We went to the kitchen to clean up. Except we didn't stay there. Giggling like school children, we snuck to the giant industrial elevator and closed the gate. Only, I'd forgotten how loud the motor was.

As the elevator slowly started to descend, our friends surrounded the cage and started throwing flower petals on us. We laughed as they teased us for sneaking off, and I kissed my bride as a flurry of white rose petals showered down around us.

Like I said.

It was perfect.

ABOUT THE AUTHOR

Thank you for reading *Marked By The Devil!* If you enjoyed this book please let me know on by reviewing on Amazon and Goodreads! You can find me on Facebook, Twitter, or you can email me at: JoannaBlakeRomance@gmail.com

Sign up for my newsletter for sneak peeks, giveaways and more!

Coming soon:
   The Untouchables Book 3
   Rock Gods Book 3
   The start of a NEW series!
   And a super secret collaboration with author Bella Lovewins!

Other works by Joanna Blake:
   BRO'
   A Bad Boy For Summer
   PLAYER
   PUSH
   Go Long
   Go Big
   Cockpit

Hot Shot
Stud Farm (The Complete Delancey Brothers Saga)
Torpedo
Cuffed (The Untouchables MC)
Mean Machine (The Untouchables MC)
Wanted By The Devil (Devil's Riders MC Book 1)
Ride With The Devil (Devil's Riders MC Book 2)
Trust The Devil (Devil's Riders MC Book 3)
Dance With The Devil (Devil's Riders MC Book 4)
Dare Me (ROCK GODS Book 1)
Slay Me (ROCK GODS Book 2)

Turn the page for excerpts from Joanna Blake's *Mean Machine*, *Torpedo*, *Slay Me*, and *Cockpit*.

ACKNOWLEDGMENTS

LJ Anderson, Mayhem Cover Design
Valorie Clifton, Editing
Deposit Photos, Cover Photo
Just One More Page Book Promotions

MEAN MACHINE EXCERPT

Mason

"*N*o thank you, ma'am."

I turned away, finding something else to do that didn't put me right in front of the cougar making eyes at me. She'd made me an indecent proposal when I delivered her drink. It wasn't the first time, either.

I was behind the bar, forcing Jaken to wait tables. He'd been my bartender for years and was a damn good one. But I was the boss and I was tired of running around like a chicken without it's head.

So I pulled rank.

It was much more relaxing behind the bar. But there was just one problem. The women.

My place used to be a biker bar. I'd eased it more into a rustic country road juke joint after the drama from last year. There'd been a murder in the parking lot, and Cass had gotten dragged into it.

That's how she'd met Connor, the bastard. It's not that I didn't like him, I did. But I didn't want him to know it.

Not after he'd fallen for my girl.

Anyway, the place was much more mainstream these days.

The bikers still came in, but not in droves. Now it was more of a colorful bar with damn good food. But try telling that to the ladies.

They wanted bikers and they weren't shy about asking for what they wanted.

I was a biker, even though I wasn't active in the club. I was a member for life, whether I liked it or not. Just wearing leather and having wheels was like catnip to these chicks. So, I spend a lot of time fending off advances. Some that were not too subtle.

At the moment, it was a woman named Mag who was making eyes at me from the other end of the bar. I kept moving so she couldn't get too close. I could tell she wanted someone to get rough with her, and that had never been my idea of a good time, even back in the day.

I groaned, rubbing the back of my neck. I used to hide in my office if I got wind of a woman like Mag on the prowl. They were easy to spot, and Jaken warned me sometimes too. But until I hired more staff, that was going to be impossible.

It was still early and destined to get worse. I served another round and snuck up the stairs in the back to get some peace and quiet. I sat heavily in my old leather desk chair. It had conformed to my body over the years and was super comfortable. Almost an easy chair.

I'd even fallen asleep in it a couple of times.

Okay, more than a couple.

I had five minutes tops before I had to get back out to the floor. Jaken could run drinks and orders and man the bar for a little while. I closed my eyes and heaved a sigh of relief.

Of course, someone knocked at the door almost right away.

"Yeah?"

I tried not to sound surly but I was. I was surly.

"Boss? Someone here to see you."

"Who?"

Jaken raised his eyebrows meaningfully.

"Someone about the ad in the paper."

I sat up straight.

"Okay." Jaken turned to go but I waved him back. "Wait. Anything I should know? Does she seem crazy?"

"Not even a little."

"Anything else?"

He smiled.

"Well, let's just say that if this one falls in love with you too, you won't be complaining. I'll send her back."

I was still frowning over that last comment when I heard a soft rap at the door.

"Come in."

The door opened and time stood still. I stared at the girl standing shyly in the entryway, my hand frozen in mid-air. Long auburn hair and hazel eyes in a heartbreakingly pretty face, with a sprinkle of freckles over the bridge of her dainty, slightly upturned nose.

I wasn't thinking coherently, so that was all I saw. Until she moved. I cleared my throat and gestured to the seat.

"You can sit."

She nodded shyly and took the seat opposite my desk. I barely had time to register the threadbare coat and long legs encased in faded jeans. She was thin. Nervous. She clutched a handbag on her lap, holding on for dear life.

Like her coat, the purse was beat up. But everything else about her was fresh as a daisy. Her shiny hair, her glowing skin.

I wondered how old she was. Mid-twenties, I thought. A couple of years older than Cassie.

Her clothes had seen better days but it only made her beauty more obvious. She was flawless. Neat as a pin. But it was the serious look in her eyes that took my breath away.

This girl was not about to start professing her love for me or modifying her uniform to show off her feminine assets. She was too shy and she had too much dignity. Her eyes said it all.

And the colors. Her eyes were a rich combination of green and gray and yellow. Not dark, like hazel tended to be. They were bright, lit up like the colors of mother nature in all her glory.

They actually sparkled.

"What's your name?"

"Shell. Michelle."

Her voice was soft and melodious. Sweet and feminine and alluring. It did something to me. Made me want to lean forward and hang on every word.

The name suited her, I thought. Shells were delicate and pretty, like her. And she looked like she was the type to take long walks on the beach.

I shook my head. I had to focus. She was pretty enough to be in one of those natural beauty commercials, but she was here for a job, not to be gawked at.

"I'm Mason. This is my place."

She nodded earnestly and I felt my insides twist. I was already trying to figure out a way to let her down easy. I needed a waitress badly, but this girl was trouble. Not only was she too fragile looking for the rough crowd we got sometimes, but she would be a constant distraction to everyone who worked here.

Especially me.

Then again... Cass had handled it. She was a beautiful girl, too. And even a little younger when she worked here. Maybe it wasn't fair to discount her, just because the girl seemed so shy.

"Have you waited tables before?"

Again, she nodded. Not one for talking then. Maybe that wasn't a bad thing.

"What kinds of places?"

"A couple of diners, a sports bar, and a chain place. You know, endless bread bowls"

I smiled at that.

"Are they really endless?"

She bit her lip and shrugged. Obviously, my jokes were not landing. I felt like a damn fool, truth be told.

I leaned back in my chair, feeling like my insides were all twisted up. I had to get rid of her. I'd scare her off, then I wouldn't have to be mean. That would be best for everyone.

"This place can get pretty rough sometimes. Especially late at night. Think you can handle it?"

She nodded. This time I raised my eyebrows, encouraging her to answer me. She was making me nervous. I needed to know she could speak.

Plus, I wanted to hear her voice again.

"I can. Handle it, I mean."

She held up her keychain. Pepper spray. I looked at her eyes quickly, seeing something there I didn't like.

She had seen trouble before, without a doubt.

"You run into a problem out there? Somebody messing with you?"

She shrugged.

"No. Just working late shifts. I've had a few close calls."

It chilled my blood, the thought of someone trying to hurt this beautiful girl. It really did.

"I hope you don't think that's enough to protect you if someone really wants to hurt you."

I sounded like her father. Or a cop, for God's sake. I was seriously fucking furious that someone had bothered this beautiful, delicate looking girl.

She smiled and I inhaled, holding my breath. It felt like the sun came out. My office wasn't dark anymore. The day wasn't overcast anymore outside the window behind me.

Or at least, it felt that way.

"I know. I always ran. But I had this ready just in case."

"Good."

I made the decision without thinking. I just opened my mouth and the words came out.

"Pay is eight bucks an hour, plus tips. You keep all of those. We are short staffed so you can work as much as you want. We'll feed you, one meal per shift. And you can take a fifteen minute break every couple of hours, as long as it's not super busy. Sound good?"

"Yes. Sounds great."

"You just need to fill out some paperwork and we'll get you in the payroll system. Do you have photo ID?"

She nodded eagerly and fished in her bag for her wallet. I felt my gut turn over when she pulled it out. A popular cartoon character was printed on the front.

She was a kid. Just a kid.

So why was I fantasizing about pulling her onto the desk and having my way with her?

She was holding her ID out to me expectantly, I realized. I glanced at the card, clocking her age. Mid-twenties, thank God.

I might be acting like a lech, but at least I wasn't a dirty old man.

"I just need to make a copy of this."

She nodded, looking so relieved that I almost cried. She must be in dire straights. I glanced at her shoes on the way out of the office to the copy machine in the hallway.

Yep. Just as I thought. They were lace up booties, scuffed up like crazy. The girl was on hard times. But she had pulled herself together nicely, all the same.

I made a photocopy of her ID for her file, then hit the button and made another. This one I folded up and put in my pocket. I couldn't have told you why I did that though.

"Here you go."

I handed her back her ID, then pulled a t-shirt from a box in the corner.

"Is small okay?"

She nodded, clutching the t-shirt against her like it was a baby. I frowned again, deciding I was going to get to the bottom of who this girl was, and what was going on with her.

"So, when can you start?"

A huge smile lit up her face. It hit me like a punch to the gut. My chest felt like it cracked open, but it didn't hurt. It felt fucking amazing.

Her beauty literally overwhelmed me.

I realized in that moment I had made a very big mistake. Huge. Monumental.

"Right now, if that's okay. I just need to run out to my car."

I nodded and she was off like a shot. I blinked a few times once she was gone. Then I reached for the bottle of bourbon I kept on my desk and poured myself a drink. I had a feeling I was going to need it.

"Mason, you are a bona fide idiot."

TORPEDO EXCERPT

Gabe

"*H*mmfff, this is good."

I grinned at the gorgeous girl who was staring out the window. She was trying not to look at me, I realized. To give me privacy so I could eat.

It was considerate.

But I didn't like it.

Not one bit.

And this sandwich *was* damn good. Delicious even. She'd done something with basic turkey and made it delicious. Avocado, tomato and sliced onions. A touch of mustard and... I think she'd put a little salt and vinegar on the veggies.

I smacked my lips.

Yep, that was it. Oil and vinegar. That's the kind of sandwich you got in an authentic Italian cafe. I looked at her with newfound respect. Tabitha was full of surprises.

The girl could *cook*.

I let my eyes travel over her curves, wondering what else she could do. That led to a couple of visual images that were definitely not PG. Or even PG 13. More like R verging on those soft-core movies they showed late at night on certain cable channels.

The 'movies' with the terrible actors and actresses with fake boobs. There was nothing fake on Tabitha though. I licked my lips, looking her over.

Hmmmfff... not one damn thing. I tilted my head to the side, trying to imagine her naked. And smiling. And-

"Are you okay?"

Tabitha ran across the room and thwaked me on the back. I coughed out the bite I'd been slowly chewing. I had not been choking. I had simply been distracted by her bodacious-

"Gabe!"

She was staring at me, reaching for my mouth. I realized she was going to start manually clearing my air pipe in about three seconds if I didn't say anything. I guess she was a pretty good nurse after all. Or nurse-in-training.

"I'm fine!"

I was, however, hard as a rock. Tabby was kneeling between my knees, her hands on my thighs. It was an almost-about-to-give-head position. I stared at her, my eyes devouring her. I wanted to remember this moment, for later.

She smelled so good, like vanilla and cinnamon. She looked even better than she smelled, with her wide eyes and creamy skin, those gorgeous lips of hers parted unconsciously. It was too much. I felt my cock lurch in response.

I moaned. Loudly.

She leaned back, moving her hands away from my knees.

"Did I hurt you?"

"No. I just-"

I grabbed a magazine and dropped it on my lap.

"I'm fine."

She looked at me suspiciously, as if she knew I was lying. Or kind of lying. I *was* fine other than having a nuclear warhead in my pants. But she knew something was up.

Clearly, Tabitha's bullshit-o-meter was a finely tuned piece of equipment.

That didn't surprise me actually. She hadn't had an easy time of it back in high school. From what I could tell, the guys were always after her but she didn't have a lot of friends.

She had a reputation as kind of a tough girl actually.

She didn't look tough to me though. She never had. She looked... just over it. The girl was not easily impressed. I realized we had that in common.

"So, what *have* you been up to? Since high school?"

She narrowed her eyes at me. I could see her chewing the inside of her cheek. It made me want to yank her down on my lap and-

"This isn't a social call, Gabe. I'm here to take care of you."

I held up my hands and smiled cajolingly. Thankfully the magazine didn't slip. That would have been embarrassing.

And it would have ruined the plans I was making. My dirty mind was very, very busy today. First, I had plans to get her in bed, and then I had lots of ideas what to do once I had her there.

My earlier resistance to having her as my aid was rapidly fading. No, I did not want this ridiculously hot woman seeing me like this. But maybe I could use it to my advantage.

Gain her sympathy and all that.

Besides, I never backed away from a challenge.

Somehow, having her resist my attempts to draw her out was making me even more determined. She couldn't be more appealing if she was covered in whipped cream with cherries on top.

But she wasn't making it easy. Tabby was a tough nut to crack. I could not stop myself from wanting to crack her shell wide open.

As annoying as it was to be stuck in a wheelchair, I was

going to use whatever I could to get Tabby in my bed. I was going to get this girl, once and for all. Not just once or twice either. I wanted a year long fuck-a-thon. Maybe longer.

I'd have to soften her up first though. I smiled to myself, thinking that wouldn't be a problem. I knew how to charm someone when I needed to.

By the time I was walking, she'd be at my beck and call.

"But I need to stay in good spirits. Isn't that part of healing? I thought I read that fifty percent of all healing was mental."

I gave her a sad look.

"I'm... lonely. Stuck down here by myself. I'm just asking you to talk, not for your hand in marriage."

She stared at me, her eyes searching. She glanced at her watch. Then she shrugged.

"Okay, fine. You don't need to take any pills for a few more hours. What do you want to talk about?"

I leaned back in my seat, mentally rubbing my hands together. And then undressing her. And then-

"I wondered what happened to you after high school. Fill me in."

She looked more than a little uncomfortable, but I didn't care. I was curious. And it wasn't like I was going to tell anyone.

"What do you want to know?"

I smiled.

"Everything."

SLAY ME EXCERPT

Nick

"*I*'d like to thank my fans..."

Nick stared bleary eyed at the golden statue in his hands as the crowd went absolutely wild.

"For this award."

He leaned toward the busty blond pop star who was presenting.

"What's the award for, doll?"

She said something and he made a face, unable to hear a word of it over the crowd.

"Well, I can't hear a fucking word you said. So, thank you for this award for the biggest fucking cock in rock and roll!"

He held it up and the crowd exploded. He grabbed his shaft through his leather pants and tugged on it. The screaming got even louder, if that was possible.

The lights dimmed and he started to wander offstage until he felt someone take his arm. He stumbled offstage and followed the signs to the greenroom.

He needed another drink.

"Here love, would you do something with this for me?"

The girl standing by the velvet rope gave him a dazzling smile and accepted the statue.

He grabbed a shot of tequila from the VIP lounge bar, dropping a fifty for the bartender. Drinks were free, but he always tipped the help. He grinned, throwing the lemon over his shoulder.

Slow clapping from the corner caught his attention. Fucking Bruce. The biggest pain in the ass alive and one of his best friends.

Hell, he was one of his *only* friends. His band. His mates from school. Kendall and Bruce.

Everyone else was just a walk-on.

"Well done."

Nick tipped his drink, sloshing most of it down his forearm. He licked his hand and chugged the rest of the shot. He held his hand out and the glass was magically refilled.

"Thanks, mate."

He swaggered across the room. Bruce watched him, an amused look on his handsome face.

"Congrats on the prize. The speech, not so much."

"What are you so happy about, you smug bastard?"

Bruce's expression cleared and Nick kicked himself mentally. Bruce was not happy. They both knew it.

He hadn't been happy in a long time.

Nick knew he had his reasons, but to be that rich and famous and such a sourpuss... what a fucking waste. Still, Bruce had been famous longer than any of the three friends, and Nick knew it was wearing on him.

Nick had his own way of handling the stress and strain of megastardom. Mostly alchohol and female companionship. He slapped Bruce's back, determined to cheer his friend up.

He just needed a little... perspective.

"You know what your bloody problem is?"

"What?"

"You need to drink more."

He downed his shot and waved for another.

"Bring two!"

"I'm not drinking tonight."

"Right, right. More for me."

"Drinking isn't the answer to anything, Nick."

"You're such a mother hen."

Bruce just raised an eyebrow, cool and collected as always.

"If you don't want to drink, at least pop off with someone. You need to get laid, mate."

That was the wrong thing to say apparently. Bruce stood to go.

"Hey wait mate, I didn't tell you about Kendall."

"Okay, tell me."

"He's got this bird, mate. Fit. Not one of us."

"She's not in the biz?"

"She's a civilian, mate."

"We told him to keep it to the industry. Everyone else is just a fan."

"He doesn't think so. He's moved her in with him."

Bruce exhaled.

"Is he happy?"

"As a lark."

Nick made some whistling sound, like a couple of love birds.

"Then leave it alone."

"Yeah, yeah. I have no one to go out trolling for chicks with now."

Bruce laughed, shaking his head.

"You always said the women come to you."

"They do. Course they do."

Bruce held out his hand and Nick stood to shake it.

"You know, some people actually want more out of life Nick."

Nick had no idea what to say to that. His friend was getting deep as the years rolled on. They used to get wild together. Now Kendall was settling down and Bruce was turning into a Buddhist Monk or something.

"You're fucking wise, mate."

Bruce just shook his head.

"No. I'm not. I'm just tired. Enjoy your night."

Nick grinned.

"Always, mate."

Nick partied the rest of the night with a couple of girls he met at one of the after parties. When he woke up at three o'clock the following day, he couldn't even remember their names.

COCKPIT EXCERPT
Jagger

*M*arines from all over the camp crowded around me as I dug into my trunk. My unit was going home, so I was giving my goodies away along with the rest of the guys. All the stuff that made living in the ass end of the world bearable.

Skin mags. Smokes. Booze. A couple of dog-eared paperback novels. An unopened bag of socks my foster sister had sent. Dice.

I even had a set of checkers.

I was keeping my lucky deck of cards though.

"And to you K-Dawg, I bequeath my prized possession. Racy redheads."

I made a big show of handing Ken the magazine that had gotten me through a lot of lonely nights. I had a thing for redheads now. Ever since her.

The fallen angel.

Sweet Jenny, whatever her last name was.

The picture I liked the best was one of a girl from the back. All you could see was her red hair and the curve of her ass. It almost looked like her. The one that had got away. It was a damn shame too.

I'd thought about her the whole damn time I was overseas. I was tempted to go back to that base and try and track her down, even though it was two states away from my next assignment.

I'd look like an idiot walking into a bar and asking about a girl with no last name that I'd met a year and a half ago.

Fuck though, after the night we'd had it might be worth it.

"Do I need gloves for this? Or maybe a hazmat suit?"

"No K-Dawg. I jack off into a condom."

"What the fuck for?"

"Reminds me of the real thing dude."

I reached into my trunk and pulled out a roll of rubbers.

"Speaking of which."

I tossed them into the crowd. The guys grabbed at them, acting like lunatics. Not that many of them were going to get laid over here. They'd probably end up making balloon animals out of them. But I knew they had to let off steam anyway they could.

Hell, I did too.

Gambling, running laps around the perimeter of the encampment, or just thinking about what I was going to do when I got back to the states.

This time it was for good. My unit was being sent back. But I was going to be a pilot trainer for the duration of my service. For some reason, the powers that be had thought I would be good at it.

It would be a big change, but I was ready for it.

Truth be told, I was tired.

"I'm going to miss you fuckers."

It was true. That was the only hard thing about this. My unit was going home, but I had other friends here. Leaving these guys to face God knows what without me felt like I was cutting off a hand with a rusty saw.

Still, not getting shot at was going to be a nice change of pace.

Not that I was going to do what everybody else did. I'd seen it time and again. Single guys left and then the next thing you knew, they were popping out babies left and right. Even Joss had done it. The iceman himself had fallen in love with a pop star of all things, gotten hitched and started procreating.

If he could crack under pressure, then the rest of these guys were toast. They might as well start picking out table-cloths. I, on the other hand, had things to do.

Manly things. Things with women. With hard drinking. With my bike.

I wanted to ride cross-country, hitting every juke joint I came across. I got a little misty eyed thinking about it.

Hell, maybe I'd even find my little redhead.